Acknowledgments

I sincerely want to thank Mrs. Rebecca Seevers for her time, advice and editing skills. We all need help along the way, and Miss Rebecca filled that role for me.

I would also like to acknowledge the following:

Samantha and Michael Case for designing the cover. I gave them the premise of the book and was blown away by the interpretation. Young people with skills are a joy to behold.

JT Hardcastle for his help putting the front and back covers together.

Becky Kelly for sharing her military life experience.

My wife Donna for her sacrifice of my little free time to write this story.

To the men who have influenced my life through athletics: I cannot tell you how much I appreciate what you have taught me about hard work, perseverance and teamwork. God has used you in a mighty way for so many.

This story is fictional, but the names used were some of the many people who have crossed my path in my sixty years. I truly enjoyed incorporating them in the story.

When It Rains

By Darrell Hardcastle

Chapter 1

California Babe Ruth Baseball Commissioner Pete Moreno stepped up to the podium and spoke into the microphone. "And now ladies and gentlemen, I have the honor of announcing the Most Valuable Player of the California State fourteen-year-old baseball tournament. I can honestly say that I wouldn't be surprised to see this young man wearing a professional uniform someday." Moreno continued, "From Fairfield, Don Kelly."

As Don made his way to the podium, the audience in the Holiday Inn Banquet Hall rose to their feet in appreciation of the young Kelly's performance during the tournament. The six foot fourteen-year-old had broken several state records while leading his team to the State Championship.

Lt. Colonel James Kelly watched with pride as his son accepted his plaque. His six foot two inch, 220 pound frame was imposing in his dress blues.

"Excuse me, sir," came a voice from behind. James turned to face a well-built man wearing a white polo shirt with a Bengal Tiger patch on his chest. "My name is Russell Best. I'm the head baseball coach at Pacific University." The two men shook hands as Best continued, "I watched your son this week, and I've got to tell you, I'm really impressed with, not just his talent, but also with his attitude and maturity." The comment drew a smile from the Lt. Colonel. "Will he be attending Vanden High this year?" asked the coach.

"I'm afraid not. I've got orders to go to Sheppard Air Force Base in Texas next month."

Coach Best reached into his pocket and handed James his card. "I was hoping to get a chance to watch him during his high school career. If I could, I would offer him a scholarship right now. He's a special player.

"I appreciate you saying that, Coach," said the normally taciturn father.

1

"Please keep me posted on your movements these next few years. If your son doesn't sign a professional contract, I would love for him to be a Tiger. The two men shook hands. "Thank you for your service, sir."

As Coach Best headed for the door, Don was making his way back to the table. "Congratulations, son," said James as he hugged Don. "We have a long drive back home, so we had better get going."

As the Lompoc Holiday Inn got smaller in the rear view mirror, the elder Kelly replayed the conversation with Coach Best to his son. "You know Donnie, that's quite an honor to be told that at your age. You have done a great job enhancing the gift you were given." James paused for a moment, "Your Granddaddy Floyd told me something that I would like to pass on to you. He told me that being an athlete was what I did; it wasn't who I was." Taking his eyes off the road to look at his son, James asked, "Do you know what he meant by that Donnie?"

Don's thoughtful response made his father smile. "If being an athlete is who I am, then who will I be if I am no longer an athlete?" Don paused, then asked, "Is that why our family verse is Colossians 3:23?"

"Yes, Donnie. Whatever you do, honor God." James took the next exit and pulled into a Shell station, got out, and left Don to his thoughts.

After filling up, the Kelly boys were back on the road for the remaining five hour drive back to Travis Air Force Base. Don grabbed a pillow from the back seat of the extended cab, reclined the passenger seat, and got comfortable.

After a couple of minutes, Don sat up and asked, "Dad, how do you honor God?"

"Well, I was taught to honor God three ways: First, by being generous with my time and money."

Don interrupted, "Is that why I always see you doing stuff for those people at the old folks' home?"

2

James chuckled, "It's actually a retirement community, but yes, there are several widows and retired vets living there. Our culture, unfortunately, tends to forget our elderly." James could tell his son was waiting for him to continue. "The second way is by excellent effort in whatever I am doing, and the third is by keeping my attitude right regardless of what is happening in my life, good or bad."

James continued to navigate the Highway 101 traffic. "That last one has been the most difficult. I sometimes struggle with how bad things still happen to those who try to honor God with their lives. The loss of your mother is a great example."

"What's the answer to that, Dad?"

"When I asked my father, the same question, he simply said, *"When it rains, everyone gets wet."* He also reminded me that, even though I tried to honor God, I fell short, which was the reason for the Cross in the first place."

The two rode in silence for several seconds. "That makes sense. Thanks, Dad." Don lay back down and was asleep in minutes.

Lt. Colonel Kelly took a long sip from the coffee he purchased at the station. He looked over at his son and noticed the plaque lying between them. With the traffic thinning out, he allowed himself to reflect on the many days he and Don had played ball together. The season determined the ball they played. As Donnie grew, the elder Kelly could tell that his son had inherited the Kelly athleticism.

James had married his childhood sweetheart, Becky Todd, before his junior year at Ole Miss. Their five year fairy tale marriage had a tragic ending, when Becky died giving birth to Don. Since that day, he devoted his life to his son and his country. He still ached for the one who captured his heart nearly twenty years prior.

He grew up in the small town of Clarksdale, Mississippi. An All State running back and kicker, James signed with the University of Mississippi and played defensive back. At 6'2" and 205 pounds, he was more suited for safety. Kelly was known to be a tenacious defender who loved contact. He found himself in the Ole Miss record books the day he intercepted 3 passes against Arkansas.

As talented as number 25 was, his dream was to be an Air Force pilot. He chose the University of Mississippi ROTC program to pursue that dream. After graduation he and Becky headed for Lackland Air Force Base in San Antonio, Texas.

It was 11 p.m. when James saw the sign indicating they were just outside Santa Cruz. The sign jogged his memory about the time his parents, Floyd and Ellie, took him to Santa Cruz Beach and Boardwalk on a trip to California. It would be the last vacation he would take with his intact family of three, and the proximity to that special place caused him further reflection.

After graduation Floyd, who had been an excellent baseball player in his day, turned down a minor league contract with the St. Louis Cardinals to join the military. After basic training, Floyd and Ellie were married in their home church in Clarksdale. They were both 18 at the time. James was born just under a year later. Later, after two miscarriages, Ellie had had a hysterectomy, at the age of 23, leaving young James an only child.

Floyd and Ellie had met at the Baptist Church in Clarksdale the summer before their senior year. Ellie had moved there

4

with her mother after her father died. They eventually started sitting next to each other on the back pew. It was there that they held hands for the first time. From that day on, they would hold hands while listening to the sermon by Pastor Dennis Henderson. Ellie had a beautiful singing voice. Sometimes Floyd would lip sync just to listen to her sing those old hymns. The death of her father had drawn her nearer to God, and she always felt better when she was singing.

After Army Basic Training, Floyd Kelly was sent to Fort Polk, Louisiana, for infantry school. Eventually he was to leave the Fort, also known as, Tigerland, for a yearlong tour in Vietnam. The young couple decided it would be best if Ellie and baby James moved to live with her widowed mother in Clarksdale.

Upon his return to the States, Floyd was accepted to Flight School to be a Warrant Officer Helicopter Pilot. He had proven to be highly intelligent, trustworthy, and intrepid--all qualities befitting a pilot who would be under fire.

Ellie and James met Floyd at Fort Wolters just outside Mineral Wells, Texas. By now little Jim was walking and talking. After he got used to the 'strange' man in his house, he fell in love with his daddy. Whenever Floyd had time, he would spend it with his family. Every Sunday they could be found at the Base Chapel for church service, holding hands in the back pew.

After completion of his training on the Huey, Warrant Officer Kelly was to be sent back to Vietnam. He drove his family back to Mississippi and found it much more difficult this time, leaving his little boy and his bride. The life expectancy for Huey Pilots was not optimal.

Over the next three years, Captain Floyd Kelly logged over 1100 combat hours. He, like other pilots, was asked to put himself in harm's way on nearly every mission. He was awarded the Distinguished Flying Cross, the Silver Star, and 29 Air Medals. He also earned a Purple Heart when he was shot down in a rescue attempt of another downed crew. A bullet shattered his right knee effectively ending his military career.

Floyd opened a body shop in Clarksdale and coached James in Little League baseball. Ellie's mother died when James was 12. Exactly one year to the day, James found his father on the floor of his shop dead from a brain aneurism.

"Hey, Dad, I need to go," a sleepy Don said from his reclined position.

"We're about 10 minutes from home son. You must have really been tired. You slept nearly the whole way home." A few minutes later, James pulled onto the driveway and turned off the engine. He grabbed the MVP plaque and made a fist with his right hand. Don smiled, made his own fist and bumped his dad's. "You were outstanding, Donnie."

"Thanks, Dad."

6

Chapter 2

With three weeks remaining before he had to report to Sheppard AFB, Lt. Colonel Kelly seized the opportunity to spend time with his mother Ellie who lived just three hours away from the base. Don loved his grandmother dearly and enjoyed her place in the country.

When James had been a junior in high school, he had accompanied his mother on a trip to Van Alstyne to visit a friend who lived there. Ellie had fallen in love with the charming little town, and James liked it too. He had decided then that if he could ever afford it, he would buy his mother a home in the north Texas community. Therefore, when he made Captain, he had purchased a small house outside of town. The house sat on 10 wooded acres with a barn and a pond.

Every vacation father and son would make the trip to Texas. James took advantage of "Mimi's Place" by teaching Donnie how to use a chainsaw and splitting axe. His desire to teach his son about hard work paid off for Ellie. The boys would cut wood, clear brush, and fix fences along with any other house maintenance needed. They also fished the pond nearly every day. Ellie was a great cook which made the Kelly boys very happy. A visit to Mimi's Place usually meant leaving a couple of pounds heavier.

As they pulled onto the long gravel driveway, Don could see Ellie on the wraparound porch sitting on her swing. She had her customary mason jar of sweet tea in her hand. Don was the first out of the truck. "Boy, you are growing like a weed."

"Hi, Mimi, got any more tea?" asked Don while giving her a hug.

"You know I do. It's on the table; ice is already in the glass. I know my grandson," she said confidently.

James put a bear hug on his mother lifting her off the ground. "Hey, Momma, good to see you."

A barely audible, "I can't breathe," came out of Ellie's mouth.

They both started laughing as James set her down on the porch.

"You look great, Mom, how are you?"

"I'm well, son. Come in the house; dinner is on the table." Mother and son walked arm in arm into the small two story house.

After three weeks full of good food, hard work, cards, and laughter, it was time for the Lt. Colonel to report to Sheppard AFB. Don still had two weeks before he was to report for his freshman year in football. James knew he would be busy so they decided that Ellie would bring him to Wichita Falls in ten days. After Mimi's breakfast of eggs, potatoes, bacon, and biscuits, the elder Kelly loaded his truck and headed for his new assignment.

Chapter 3

"Mimi, I'm going for a run," Don yelled as he headed out the door. Wearing running shoes, black shorts, and an Ole Miss t-shirt, he headed to the gravel road that ran adjacent to Ellie's property. The early morning Texas heat was already starting to become evident. Don had been running every morning since his arrival. His 6' frame carried 160 pounds.

It was obvious he had the Kelly DNA. James had taught his son a lot about athletic preparation. Donnie would often work out with his father. Whether it was running, lifting weights, or self-defense, it was clear that he possessed the family competitiveness. After a thirty-minute run, Don headed for the barn to climb the 20 foot rope he and his father hung two years prior. After two trips up the rope, he spent ten minutes punching and kicking the heavy bag and five more on the speed bag, which were installed a year before the rope.

Lieutenant Colonel Kelly had spent his entire forty years in good physical condition. He enjoyed using his body weight in his exercise routine. James believed that if he were in great physical condition, his men would be challenged to strive for the same standard. He was a master at hand-to-hand combat, despite the fact that he was a fighter pilot. James taught Don self-defense to build confidence and mental toughness. He also believed it taught Donnie how to react calmly under pressure. Personally, the Colonel used the workouts for mental and physical agility.

The only time James had to use his training was when he and Becky were out on a date many years before. The young Lieutenant came out of the restroom at a crowded Charlie's Bar and Grill in San Antonio, Texas, to find three locals at his table. One of them was sitting a little too close to his beautiful bride. James looked at Becky's face and could see the fear in her eyes. "Excuse me, gentlemen, can I help you?" His eyes were set on the man in the chair.

The seated man stood, which told James he was outsized. The tattooed giant stood 6'5 and weighed around 250 pounds. The other two were closer to the Lieutenant's size. It was obvious they had spent more time at the 'bar' part of Charlie's. "No, you, can't," said the bigger man. "I'm more interested in what this pretty little lady can do for me," he said, as he placed his large paw on Becky's shoulder, drawing a laugh from the two at his snarky response.

Continuing his shark eye stare, James said in a barely audible voice, "Sir, that's my wife, and you will get your hand off her."

The large man grinned and moved toward James. "What are you going to .... "

Before he could finish his sentence, a lightning strike to the throat left the big man gasping for air on Charlie's Bar and Grill floor. The lieutenant turned to the other two men. He could see the trepidation in their eyes. The one closest to him raised his hands to indicate his lack of desire to join the fray. James reached out to his bride and took her trembling hand. "Gentlemen, you might want to check on your friend."

After Don finished his time on the speed bag, he headed for the house. The coolness of the air conditioning was a welcome change. He opened the fridge to find a fresh pitcher of sweet tea. He filled the Mason jar twice before he closed the refrigerator door. "Mimi, I'm back," yelled her grandson, not knowing if his grandmother was in the house.

"I'm upstairs, Donnie. Come on up. I want to show you something."

When he reached his Mimi's room, Don found her sitting on the bed. She had a large shoe box next to her. "Did you buy me some cowboy boots?" he quipped.

"No I didn't, but now that you are a Texan, I might have to do just that." She continued, "I was in the attic looking for something, and I found this box. I forgot I had it."

"What's in it, Mimi?" her curious grandson asked trying to peek inside.

"It's mostly stuff I've kept from your daddy's childhood. Let's take a look and see what we have," she said as she dumped the contents onto the bed. Don placed his tea on the nightstand and sat on the bed with his back on the headboard. He grabbed some pictures while Ellie was reading old letters and cards. The pictures showed his father in various stages of life.

"Sweet truck," blurted Donnie as he showed Ellie a picture.

She smiled, "That was your grandfather's pride and joy." The truck was a maroon '69 Ford F-100 short bed. It had wide tires with chrome rims and baby moons. "That's your daddy sitting next to your grandfather. He was five or six at the time. Floyd bought the truck on your daddy's first birthday. He told me that he was going to give it to your daddy on his sixteenth birthday."

"Did Dad ever get the truck?" inquired a curious Don.

Ellie's countenance changed as she answered her grandson. "When your granddaddy died, I only had enough insurance to bury him, so I had to sell the truck. Your daddy was pretty torn up about it. He tried to be a man about the situation, but I could tell he was bothered.

Don looked again at the picture and asked, "Who did you sell it to?"

"Your grandfather had a friend who loved the truck and would always ask Floyd to sell it to him. He owned Haro Road Construction Company out of Memphis. Doug Haro had a thing for Ford products. At the time, he had a nine car garage full of different Ford vehicles. Mr. Haro exhibited his generosity by giving us $2,000 more than the blue book suggested. That money sustained us until I got a job at Landry's Clothiers." Donnie returned to the pictures when he noticed Ellie still lost in the memory.

The silence was broken minutes later when Don showed his grandmother an old picture of his father and another boy. They were dressed in football uniforms with WILDCATS written across the front. James Kelly was wearing number 25 while the other boy was donning the number 8. "Who's the guy with Dad?"

His Mimi looked at the picture for a second, "Oh, sweetie, that's Riley Joe. He was your dad's best friend in high school."

"You almost look sad, Mimi. Did something happen?"

Ellie grabbed Don's tea and handed it to him. "This might take a while." Mimi began, "Riley and your dad met when the Sprowls moved to Clarksdale the summer before their sophomore year. Your daddy struggled with granddaddy's death. He was rebellious and got into trouble."

Don's interest piqued, "What kind of trouble, Mimi?"

"Nothing too serious. Once during his freshman year, Officer Barnes brought him home drunk as a skunk. His son Jordan was the star varsity running back. I think Officer Barnes felt sorry for James, and he liked Floyd. Your dad was on the freshmen football team, so Barnes decided to bring Jimmy home instead of locking him up. Your daddy threw up all night. I made him get up at six in the morning and do work around the house. Let's just say, it was a long day for him." Don chuckled at his grandmother's comment. "I was nervous at the direction he was headed until he met Riley. RJ had a great head on his shoulders. He was a hard working young man with a great heart. He even had enough influence on your dad to get him

12

back in church."

Don took another drink from his tea while Ellie repositioned herself on the bed. "I'll be honest Donnie; your dad lost a lot of his drive when his daddy died. He didn't put the same effort into things as he did when Floyd was alive. Let me tell you, his coaches were frustrated to the nth degree. Because of his athleticism, he still played but not to his potential. That all changed during the winter of their junior year, and Riley was the reason." Don was looking at his grandmother with great anticipation. She took the picture of the boys and quietly stared at it, lost in the memory. "Your dad, Riley, and another friend were sledding when Riley hit a pole and was paralyzed."

A stunned look came over Don's face. "I've never heard this story, Mimi."

Ellie continued, "That day changed your dad's life. The way Riley handled the accident was nothing short of amazing. The first words to his mother were, "It's okay Mom; God has a plan."

"Wow!" was all that Don could say.

"Riley Joe was in the hospital in Memphis for 3 months. Your dad drove the 90 minutes every chance he could. On one visit Riley told your dad, "Don't waste your opportunities." From that day on, your dad was unstoppable. He even wrote RJ's statement on an index card and put it on the mirror in the bathroom as a daily reminder.

Coach Brown allowed James to wear Riley's number 8 that year in football. I'll never forget the last game of the year. Riley's parents brought him to the game in a wheelchair. By that time, he had mobility in his upper torso. The doctors originally said he only had a 5% chance of any mobility. They obviously didn't know Riley Joe. His body was undersized, but his heart wasn't. Also, there were hundreds of people praying for him, which didn't hurt either. When Jimmy saw them roll into the stadium during pre-game, he ran over to Riley. That's when I realized James was wearing his number 25. He had RJ's jersey tucked into the back of his pants. When he pulled it out and gave it to Riley, I started to cry in the stands." Mimi's eyes were tearful as she relived the moment.

Don took another drink of tea while his grandmother wiped her eyes with a tissue she had tucked in her bra strap. "Don't stop, Mimi. Tell me what happened next."

Ellie smiled and continued. "I saw your dad hug Riley's parents and then take the handles of the chair. He wheeled his best friend to the sidelines where he was mobbed by his teammates. I teared up again when James wheeled Riley out to the center of the field for the coin toss. When the boys turned back toward their sidelines, they were met with the home side fans standing. We all knew that RJ hated the limelight, so no one was clapping.

"Really, no one?"

"I know, it does seem strange, but it was a small, tight community, and in those days every parent knew every kid."

"That's pretty cool. I get chill bumps thinking about what that must have looked like," Donnie said while rubbing his arms. "Did they win the game?"

"Boy, did they! Your dad scored 5 touchdowns that night. I never saw him play better. After the game, Coach Brown gave Riley the game ball signed by the team." Ellie took a deep sigh and said reflectively, "That was a good night."

Mimi Kelly came back to the present, "Let's go downstairs, and I'll make you a sandwich." Ellie scooped up the memorabilia and tossed them back into the box. She slipped a letter into the back pocket of her Levi's. "I'll let you take the box with you to your dad's, so you can look through it at your convenience."

"You're a great Mimi; I love you," said Don while giving her a big hug before she headed downstairs.

Ellie made lunch while Don showered. As he was coming down the stairs, he could hear his grandmother singing 'Amazing Grace.' Even at 60, she still had a beautiful singing voice. She sang at her local church and was an occasional soloist.

When Don reached the table, he found a grilled cheese sandwich and a bowl of Ellie Kelly's chili. "Mmm, my favorite," he said rubbing his hands together. Ellie brought his glass of tea and sat down with him to eat. After Ellie's prayer, Don dug into the chili.

His grandmother was the only consistent female in his life. She listened well and seemed to always have the right words for her grandson. As he was munching on his grilled cheese, he remembered the letter in her pocket. "Mimi, what did you put in your pocket upstairs?"

Her response had a touch of melancholy. "Oh, Donnie, it was the last letter your granddaddy wrote to me. I was going to read it tonight in my room because I cry every time.

"Do you still miss him?" asked Don sincerely.

"Oh, sweetie, I miss him as much now as I did the day he passed."

"How old was he when he died?"

"We were both 33."

"Dad said he had a brain aneurism. Isn't 33 kind of young for that to happen?" questioned Don.

"The doctors surmised that flying under constant stress may have been a factor. They never could say for sure."

"Mimi, why didn't you get married again?

Ellie paused for several seconds, "Your grandfather was my one and only love. I had friends in Clarksdale who would set me up with dates. I always compared them to Floyd, which wasn't fair to them. When I moved here, my friend Vonda introduced me to a couple of nice men, but it just didn't click."

Don asked, "Are you lonely?"

"Not really. My friends keep me busy, and I'm active in our seniors group at church."

"I wish I could have known Granddaddy. Dad says he was a good man."

"Oh, he was, Donnie. He was rough around the edges and

15

had the Kelly pride, but he softened a lot when your daddy was born."

Don still had the letter on his mind. "Could I read it sometime?" pointing at the letter Ellie had placed on the middle of the table.

She reached for the letter and handed it to her grandson. "He wasn't verbose, so it won't take long to read. I've got to go into town. You can read it while I'm gone."

Don stood on the porch as Ellie's pickup reached the gravel road. He sat down on her swing and opened the letter. It was dated January 7, 1973. The heading was 95th Evac Hospital, Da Nang, Vietnam. The letter read:

> *My Dearest Ellie,*
>
> *It won't be long now before I can hold you in my arms. I'm being told I'll be able to go home in about 2 weeks. The thought of you and little James sustained me over here. Thank you for your constant prayers. I want you to know I had God's peace on every mission. Now that my military career is over, I'm so ready to grow old with you. The quiet nights have given me the time to think about how much you mean to me. Your kindness, strength, and grace are such wonderful qualities. Watching you with James is a joy to behold. I can't wait to hold the little guy. I go to sleep at night hearing your beautiful singing voice in my head. I thank God you are mine, my love. See you soon.*
>
> *Always,*
>
> *Floyd*

Don refolded the letter and placed it in the envelope. He slowly started swinging, thinking about the man he never met. After a few minutes, Don went into the house and returned the letter to the

16

table. He walked over to the mantel where the picture of Floyd, Ellie, and 12-year-old James sat. Next to it was a picture of Floyd in his uniform. Don took the picture off the mantel and studied it. He saw his father in the picture: tall, square jaw, and determined look. He even noticed the birthmark under his grandfather's left eye. Don took his left hand and touched the same birthmark under his own eye. He smiled when he remembered his father also had the mark. For some reason, Don was encouraged by this revelation. The way his Mimi and father talked about his granddad, and what he knew about his father, gave him hope that he could become that kind of man. Don touched the image of his granddaddy and set the picture back on the mantel.

Don pulled open the desk drawer next to the fireplace. He retrieved a pencil and a 'Post it' pad and wrote "Gone Fishing" on the yellow pad. He placed it on the table, went out the back door, and headed to the barn. His fishing gear was still in the Gator utility vehicle James bought Ellie when he purchased the property. Don started the Gator and drove out to the pond which was approximately 500 yards down a sloping hill.

Over the last five years of vacations, Don and his dad heavily fished the rectangular fishing hole. At the end of every vacation, the Kelly boys would restock the pond. In Don's mind it was a wonderful cycle. He stopped the Gator next to the 20-foot dock he helped his father build two years prior. He grabbed his fishing pole, bait, and chair out of the back of the vehicle and headed for his favorite spot.

Through the years James encouraged his son to spend time alone and quiet. He would tell Donnie, "Sometimes your brain works better when you give it a chance, but you've got to get rid of the noise."

Don reached the spot, set the gear down and opened his chair. He stood next to the chair and looked around. Memories flooded his brain. The fishing hole was his classroom, and his dad was the teacher. James Kelly loved Jesus, sports, and history. Regardless the subject, he was a great storyteller. His passion kept his son mesmerized. It was on this pond that Don learned the family verse and the family slogan, *Don't Be Common.* He learned about his country and its founding fathers in ways not taught in school. James talked to Donnie about work ethic, attitude, and humility. He would often tell Don that, "A dangerous man wears a humble man's cloak." The Colonel even made Donnie memorize a quote from Homer Hickam which hung on his office wall that read, "There is no water holier than the sweat off a man's brow."

After several minutes of surveying his favorite fishing hole, Don sat down. With all of his fishing gear lying next to him, Don's mind traveled back to his most memorable day on Ellie's pond five years prior.

"Hey, Dad?" Don questioned after spending several minutes in deep thought. "You've told me a lot of stories about mom, but you never told me how you met."

"I haven't? Huh." James set his pole on a Y-shaped stick, which was stuck in the ground. "I remember the first time I saw her. My friend Paul Hayashino and I were playing ping pong in the Student Union right before school started, when a cue ball hit me in the foot. When I picked it up, there she was. She had brown hair to the middle of her back. When I gave it to her, she looked at me with those gorgeous brown eyes, smiled and said "Thank you" with a southern accent. I was toast."

Don could tell his dad was lost in the memory. "Did you ask her out?"

"No, she appeared to be out of my league," the colonel replied.

"What do you mean by 'out of my league'?" asked Don.

James laughed, "It means I didn't think she would go for someone like me."

"I don't understand. If you thought she was out of your league, how did you get married?"

James reeled in his line and checked his bait. Seeing that it was still intact, he cast the line in an area of the pond shaded by a live oak tree. "That's where chapter two comes in. After my feeble, "You're welcome," Paul and I went back to our game. I made him switch places, so I could get a better view of the brunette beauty. Needless to say, Paul smoked me that game." Donnie laughed and James continued. "Shortly after my encounter with her, she and her friend left. Something funny must have been said, because I heard her infectious laugh."

"Did she have a good sense of humor?" Don asked, while reaching into the ice chest for an iced tea.

"Son, your mother had a great sense of humor and the quickest wit. Watching a funny movie with her was pure joy."

James paused in thought, and then proceeded. "After she left the Student Union, I didn't see her again. The campus filled quickly with students moving into the dorms, and I was spending most of my time in football."

Don's pole suddenly bent. He jerked the rod and set the hook. The multiple days on the pond made him highly efficient at this maneuver. Don was reeling in what looked to be a nice size catfish.

James grabbed the net and scooped the fish. "Hey, that's a big one!"

Donnie's smile was ear to ear as he grasped the fish and took out the hook. "It looks to be about 3 or 4 pounds," said the youngster while holding up the catfish for his father to see. He placed the fish on the stringer with the other two previously caught. "It's the biggest one so far," bragged the young angler. He baited his hook and tossed it back into the water. Father and son performed their obligatory fist bump as Donnie settled back into his chair. "So when did you see mom again?" Don's curiosity was piquing.

"About a month or so later my roommate Bill asked me if I wanted to go on a double date. I had never been on a blind date before, so I asked him what she looked like. I had heard blind dates usually turned out disastrous. His reply told me this might not be the case. "Well, she was Miss Teen South Dakota last year."

"I immediately responded, 'Sure, I'll take a chance!' Don laughed at his dad's shallowness. "When I was finally introduced to the mystery girl, I was thrilled. It was the girl in the Student Union."

"Wait a minute," interrupted Donnie, "Mom was Miss Teen South Dakota?"

"Yep."

"So how did the date go?"

"It was fun. We went to a movie and then to a pizza parlor. The next morning I was walking through the Union to the mail boxes and walked right past your mother. I was so distracted with thoughts of the night before, I actually walked within inches of the real thing. I was startled out of my trance by the sound of my name. I was a freshman, so I wasn't known by many. The voice was sweet and southern; it was her."

Donnie interrupted the story again, "If she was from South Dakota, how did she have a southern accent?"

James was impressed with his son's observation. "Her father was military. Most of his assignments were in the southern states."

"Sorry, Dad, I was just curious. I want to hear the rest of the story."

"No problem. She wasn't too impressed that I could walk by her without acknowledgment less than twelve hours after our date. Don, girls don't like it when they feel they are being ignored."

"Were you ignoring her?" Don asked.

"Heck, no! I was smitten, and when you are smitten, all brain function disappears." Don chuckled. "I think she was a little insulted. I tried many times, over the years, to convince her that my mind was clouded by the one I did not see."

"That's a great story Dad." The Kelly's returned to their fishing in silence.

James looked over at his son and noticed a touch of melancholy. "Are you okay?"

Don turned toward his father. "Dad, I miss her so much, and I never met her."

"I see a lot of her in you, Donnie. Your strength, courage, and sense of humor are just a few traits you got from her. She loved you with all her heart." James let out an audible sigh. "I guess you are old enough to understand now. We were thrilled when your mom finally became pregnant. After a few months she started having complications, so she went to see the doctor." James took off his cap and wiped his forehead with his handkerchief. Mom was diagnosed with a pregnancy disorder called pre-eclampsia. When the doctor tried to stress just how much danger she was in, she stopped him; "Doctor Baker, this child WILL be born. Her tone, coupled with the conviction in her eyes, signaled the doctor to simply respond, 'Yes ma'am.'

"Your mother was a faithful woman, Don. She believed the verse that says our days are numbered. She would often say that she looked forward to being with Jesus when her time on earth was done." James cleared his throat

21

to maintain his composure. "After she gave birth to you, you were cleaned up and placed on her chest. She kissed you on the forehead and reached for my hand."

"He's beautiful," she whispered. "I have no regrets," was the last thing she said as she slipped into a coma. She went home to be with the Lord an hour later."

Donnie could not control his tears. James embraced his son for a long minute. When they broke, he said, "Let's go to the house."

Rain drops started falling on Donnie bringing him out of his memory. He had enough experience to know that the North Texas weather could change suddenly. As the intensity of the rain increased, Don picked up his pace retrieving his gear and chair. He knew that running wouldn't lessen his chances of getting soaked, so he moved deliberately to the Gator. A nearby lightning strike, quickly followed by booming thunder, motivated the young Kelly to hasten his retreat to the barn. Once inside, Donnie parked his vehicle so he could watch the storm. Life at Mimi's was pretty good for a 14-year-old boy.

Chapter 4

The ten extra days at Mimi's place went quickly. Ellie turned off the gravel road, in her late model Ford pickup, and headed for Wichita Falls to rendezvous with her son. The 140-mile drive would have them arrive around noon. "Are you looking forward to starting high school?" she asked as she merged onto highway 82.

"Yes ma'am" was his short reply. "I am a little nervous about football. I've never played before," replied Don while looking out the window at the North Texas scenery.

The progressively darkening skies prompted Ellie to turn on her lights. "I wouldn't be concerned, son. Your daddy and granddaddy were very good athletes, and you remind me of them very much." Don smiled at his Mimi's evaluation.

….

"Lieutenant Colonel Kelly," came a voice interrupting his meeting.

"Yes?" the Colonel responded.

"You have an emergency phone call, sir." James' heart started pumping furiously as he stepped out of the room. "You can use this room for privacy sir." The young airman handed the phone to the Lt. Colonel while opening the door to an adjacent room.

James took the phone, nodded to the airman, and shut the door. "This is James Kelly."

"James, it's Mom. There has been an accident. Donnie's hurt real bad."

"What happened?" asked James, using his training to remain calm.

"I'll tell you when I get there. They are taking Donnie by Care Flight to United Regional Hospital in Wichita Falls."

"Are you okay, Mom?"

"I'm in an ambulance heading to Regional as we speak. I have some stitches and a separated shoulder. I'll be alright, son. I'll meet you at the hospital."

23

"Roger that, Momma," James replied, turning off the phone.

Twenty minutes later the uniformed Lt. Colonel was standing on the top of the United Regional helipad as the Careflight helicopter landed. The hospital team went to work immediately. The Colonel knew enough not to get in the way. As they wheeled his son by him, James could see the severity of Don's injuries. His face was unrecognizable and there was a lot of visible blood. As he watched the gurney disappear, the stoic officer was talking to Jesus.

Forty-five minutes after the helicopter arrived, James Kelly's prayers were interrupted by a familiar voice, "Jimmy, how's Donnie?"

James opened his eyes to find his mother with a large bandage on her forehead and her left arm in a sling. He immediately stood and carefully hugged his mother. "He's in surgery. I haven't talked to anyone. What happened, Mom?" They both sat down on a chapel pew. Ellie's wince told James his mother was in a lot of pain.

"We were outside of Nocona, and a broken down 18-wheeler was on the side of the highway, situated right before a side road. It was raining pretty heavily, and the driver of a dump truck couldn't see us as he pulled out and hit us on Donnie's door. He was fooled by the pickup in front of us because it was the same make, model, and color as mine."

"You're kidding!" said James shaking his head.

"The driver of the truck was devastated when he saw what had happened to Donnie. He's the one who called 911. He stayed and prayed for Don until they put him in the helicopter. His name was Dan 'Trig-lee-a' I think."

"Actually it's pronounced 'Trill-ya'" came a voice from behind. A large bearded man with a *Triglia Hauling* cap in his hand stood at the back of the chapel. "I'm Dan. I came to check on the boy and to tell you how sorry I am."

The Colonel stood and faced Dan extending his hand. "James Kelly." He looked toward Ellie, "My mother shared what happened.

I appreciate you staying with my son and praying for him."

"Thank you," Dan said lowering his eyes. "When I saw the boy...."

"Don," interrupted James.

"When I saw Don's condition, praying was all I could think of doing."

A surgeon entered the chapel wearing white scrubs and a Baylor Bears scrub hat. "Colonel Kelly, I'm Dr. Charles Evans. I am the lead surgeon on your son's case. Can I talk here?" he asked, looking at Ellie and Dan.

"I can leave," said Dan.

"No, Dan, please stay," implored Ellie while touching his arm. James nodded in agreement.

"Your son is in bad shape, sir. The brain monitors are positive, but he does have head trauma. He has a nasty gash from here to here," drawing a line with his index finger starting from his forehead above his right eye in a near straight line crossing the eye socket and nose down to his lower left jaw.

"What about his eye?" asked a concerned Ellie.

"We won't know if he has vision damage until he can tell us, but we don't see any structural damage." Ellie nodded while Dan placed his large hand on her shoulder. Dr. Evans continued, "He has a transverse fracture of his right femur. Because of his multiple injuries, we did an external fixation to stabilize the leg."

"Multiple injuries?" questioned James.

"Yes sir, he also broke his right tibia and fibula which we currently have plastic casted." Looking at Doctor Evans, James could tell there was more. "Don's right humerus is broken mid shaft which has a coaptation splint. He also has 4 broken ribs, a punctured lung, bruised kidneys and a ruptured spleen." Ellie covered her mouth trying not to cry. The Lt. Colonel started to say something, but was stopped when Dr. Evans showed him his palm. "Finally sir, he has a torn MCL, PCL, and meniscus in the right knee."

James took a deep breath and blew it out all at once. "When can we see him, Doctor?" asked Ellie.

"He will be in ICU for quite a while. I couldn't tell you when he will be awake, but you can see him in about 30 minutes."

After the surgeon left the chapel, the Kellys and Dan stood silently for several moments. Finally, Dan broke the silence, "I am so sorry, sir. Is there anything you need or that I can do for either of you?"

"You can continue to pray for Donnie, Dan."

Triglia handed James his card, "Contact me if you need anything, anything at all." He added, "Would it be okay with you if I check on Don from time to time?"

"We would welcome you anytime," the Colonel responded. With that, Dan left the hospital.

James helped his mother sit back down on the front pew and placed his hand on her knee. "How are you feeling, Momma?"

"I'm physically sore and emotionally numb, son."

James looked at the cross on the wall and said aloud, "Fear not, for I am with you. Do not be dismayed, I am your God, I will strengthen you; I will help you. I will uphold you with my victorious right hand."

Ellie placed her hand on top of her son's, "Isaiah 41:10".

"That's right, Momma."

Chapter 5

"Hey, hot shot, how you doing?" James whispered to Don as he opened his eyes for the first time since the accident.

"Where am I, Dad?"

"You're in a Wichita Falls hospital, son. You and your grandmother were in a car accident."

"Is Mimi okay?" asked an instantly concerned grandson.

"She's okay. She has some stitches in her head and what turned out to be a broken collarbone." Donnie relaxed at the news about his beloved Mimi. "Don, the accident was three days ago. Do you remember anything?"

"No, Dad, I don't."

"Well, the doctor said you might not."

"Dad, what's that on my leg?" asked Don looking at the contraption holding his femur together.

"It's called an external fixator. Your femur was broken," answered James.

"I hurt everywhere, Dad."

"That's not a surprise, Donnie. You were hit by a dump truck."

Don touched his face. "What happened to my face?"

"The doctor said you must have turned toward your window, and glass cut your face on impact."

"Can I see it?"

"There's not a mirror in here, son. We'll get you one when Mimi gets here."

"How bad does it look?" Don asked, tracing the line of stitches.

"To be honest son, right now it looks bad. A plastic surgeon was brought in, and he put in nearly 100 stitches. You still have swelling, which doesn't help. The surgeon said you will have a scar, but it won't be severe. Besides, chicks dig scars," James added, trying to lessen the blow.

27

"Funny, Dad," responded Don, flashing a painful smile.

For the next several minutes, James informed his son of the extent of his injuries and what the prognosis would be for his recovery.

"Dad, why would God allow this to happen to me?" Don asked after hearing about all of the damage.

James looked at Don's tears streaming down his swollen face. "Don, do you remember when I shared your Granddaddy's saying, '*When it rains, everyone gets wet?*'" His son nodded. "It doesn't matter who they are, rich, poor, good or bad. All get wet. It happens to all of us. God never promised us a life without adversity. Think about Jesus' life. It was full of challenges. What God is most interested in, Donnie, is how we handle the adversity in our lives. We have two choices, son, when it comes to circumstances: we overcome them or they overcome us. God says He will give us what we need, when we need it. I've learned in my own life that He is true to that promise. I hope you will also learn the same."

....

Ten days later Dr. Evans allowed Donnie to go home. The Kellys decided it would be better if he stayed with Ellie during his long recovery. Donnie was wheeled to the van Ellie rented until she could replace her totaled pickup. James lifted his son into the vehicle and placed him in a back row seat. He replaced the second row seat and folded it back to front to accommodate Don's broken femur. James then placed Donnie's wheelchair in the back and slipped into the driver's seat. Ellie was already seated on the passenger side still nursing her broken collarbone.

James adjusted the rearview mirror so he could see his son's eyes. "Donnie boy, let's pretend we are in the front car of a roller coaster with our hands up. This is going to be a great adventure." After absorbing his father's message, Don raised his left arm, with a huge smile on his scarred face. Ellie also raised her good arm, followed by James raising his in solidarity. As he pulled out of the hospital parking lot, they collectively screamed like they were on a coaster's downhill slope. The loud scream was followed by robust laughter.

Nearly three hours later the Kellys pulled onto Ellie's gravel road. James parked next to Bill Castle's work truck. "They must still be here," said Ellie. "Bill and his brother Argie said they needed my key for a project they wanted to do."

Seeing a ramp leading to the porch, James asked, "Is that the project?"

"No, Dan built that. On one of his visits he asked if he could build it for Donnie. He even insisted on paying for all the materials."

"I like Dan a lot, even if he did put me in the hospital," said Don, drawing chuckles from his father and grandmother for his deadpan delivery.

After a few minutes, James was wheeling his son up the well-built ramp and into the house. Once inside, the smell of home cooking got their attention. Ellie found her friends, Vonda and Kay in the kitchen making dinner. "We thought you might be hungry, and since our husbands were here, we could kill two birds," said Vonda while receiving a hug from Ellie.

Kay added, "So we made our famous barbecue ribs, creamed corn, and green bean casserole. Oh, and by the way, we will be doing all the cooking and cleaning until you are healed Ellie; and we won't take no for an answer."

"Thank you so much, ladies. You are true friends," answered Ellie.

Argie walked into the kitchen, "Okay, break up this little lovefest. Let's eat."

Bill came out of the downstairs bedroom and addressed James, "Colonel Kelly, would you bring Donnie in here? I want to show y'all something."

James wheeled Don into the bedroom to find a clever pulley system. "Argie and I built this to make it easier for Donnie to get in and out of bed," explained Bill.

James surveyed the work, looked at Don and gave him a thumbs up. "That's fine work, gentlemen. Thank you."

"Thank you," echoed Don.

James thanked God for his provision of food and friends who show up in times of trouble. Then the friends enjoyed a time of good food and fellowship without concern for what the future might hold.

Chapter 6

James set up a rehab schedule with local physical therapist Rock King. King was a former college baseball player, which would provide instant credibility to Don. Rock offered to come by Ellie's until it was more feasible for Donnie to come to his facility.

Next, the Lt. Colonel met with the principal and counselor at the high school. They worked out a way for Don to do the work online. They also agreed that James should hire a tutor to help Don with problems and administer tests.

Knowing that he would have to return to Sheppard the next day, James spent most of the evening in his son's room. He carried Ellie's recliner into Donnie's room and positioned it so they could be face to face.

James started the conversation, "You know that it's very tenuous in the Middle East these days."

"Yes sir," replied the unusually well informed teenager.

"I have orders to go overseas to command a squadron. That will require me to be there for at least a year. You know I want to be here to help you through this."

"I know, Dad. I want you to be here too, but I understand." Don locked eyes with his father, "I want to be just like you, Dad."

"You just made my day, Donnie," his father responded.

"Anyone want some tea in there?" shouted Ellie from the living room.

"Yes ma'am," said both in unison.

"Mimi will take good care of you, Donnie, and when you are better, you can take good care of her."

Ellie entered the room with two large glasses of tea in her hand. "Here you go boys, a big glass of Ellie's famous sweet tea." Both of the Kelly boys drank nearly half the glass while Ellie watched. "I swear if you aren't two peas in a pod."

"Is that a bad thing, Mimi?" asked Don.

"No, Donnie. That's a very good thing," she said while

leaving the room.

"Okay, son, let's hear about how you are going to handle your recovery."

"I've been thinking a lot about it. First, I've accepted what happened. I also know that I have to trust Rock and do what he tells me. Finally, I'm not going to allow my circumstances to overcome me, no matter how bad it gets."

James looked at his son evaluating what he just heard. "Donnie, if anyone can overcome this adverse circumstance, it's you. When David slew Goliath, it was because he had faith in God, confidence in his abilities, and refused to listen to naysayers. If you weren't a Don, you would be a David."

"I won't let you down, Dad."

Getting up from his chair, James walked over to his pronated son and placed his forehead on his son's. "You couldn't possibly let me down, son." James kissed Don on the forehead, "I love you, son."

"Love you too, Dad."

Early the next morning, the Castle brothers arrived to take Lt. Colonel Kelly back to Sheppard AFB. They had to pick up some equipment in Amarillo, so they volunteered to take the Colonel to Wichita Falls.

On the way, they were to retrieve Donnie's belongings and the shoe box from the Nocona Salvage yard where Ellie's totaled vehicle now resided. Dan met them at the yard to get the final plans for the obstacle course he was to build for Don on Ellie's property. Dan and James had hatched the idea while having lunch at the hospital cafeteria on one of Dan's visits. James took pictures of the property and drew up plans the night before.

When Bill and Argie learned of the project, they more or less mandated their involvement. James reminded the three men that Donnie wouldn't be able to use the course for several months, so there was no need to hurry. Dan and the Castle brothers exchanged numbers and said their goodbyes.

"Colonel, may I have a word with you please?" asked Dan.

"Absolutely" responded the uniformed officer. The Castles took their cue and headed for their work vehicle.

"Sir, I was curious why you never seemed upset or angry with me for what I did to your son. Can you explain that?"

"I didn't expect that question," said a mildly surprised James. "The truth is, Dan, when my dad died, I was very angry."

"That's understandable," said Dan.

"Not really. I actually knew better, but I was an obstinate teenager who felt sorry for himself. I stopped being the person I was raised to be." Dan stood silent waiting for James to continue. "Later a good friend of mine was paralyzed in an accident. Not once did I hear him blame God, and he seemed to be at peace from the very beginning. I saw in him what I didn't see in the mirror. He changed my life. Since then, I see life differently, so I couldn't be upset or angry with you, Dan."

James placed his hand on Dan's shoulder, "It was an accident. It's just life."

Just a few miles outside of Nocona, the Castles were singing along with an old Hank Williams tune on the radio. James Kelly was seated in the back seat of the Ford F350 next to Donnie's gear and the shoe box. James opened the lid of the Tony Llama boot box and started perusing the contents. Sitting near the top were the same two pictures his son had commented on. The picture of the maroon Ford F100 brought back bittersweet memories. The memory of the day Doug Haro came from Memphis to buy it brought back a familiar pang. His father took great care of his '69. When James looked at the picture of himself and Riley, he said out loud "Riley Joe."

"Excuse me?" asked Argie, thinking he was being addressed. Kelly showed the photo to Argie, and for the last twenty minutes of the drive to Sheppard, told him of the story of the young man in the picture.

....

      The Lieutenant Colonel could feel the hot West Texas wind blowing in his face as he watched the dually disappear. He turned his attention to the large American flag waving in the wind next to the equally large Texas flag. As he gazed at the two symbols of pride and strength, James realized the two flags represented the next year of his life. His son would be rehabilitating his body here in Texas, while he would be serving his country overseas.

Chapter 7

Upon receiving his assignment to the Middle East, James Kelly also received a promotion; now he was returning home as a full Colonel. On his return flight, he switched on the overhead light above the seat, opened the satchel, and retrieved his letters. Despite technology, the Kellys always communicated via mail. It had been a year now since James had seen his son, and he looked forward to their reunion the next day. The frequently read letters told of Donnie's road to recovery from his multiple injuries.

Once Don was able, Rock King put him through a difficult, but thorough regimen. Being a former athlete himself, Rock knew the young man's needs and limitations. Don had regained 10 of the 30 pounds he lost off of his now 6'1 frame. According to Rock, Donnie was improving beyond expectations and could expect to reach his former weight of 160 pounds in two to three months.

It wasn't until James read Ellie's letters that he found out Don's progress in his school work. Ellie shared that Rebecca Seevers, the tutor, told her that Don was very well read and had a proclivity for math. Being an English teacher by trade, Seevers was most impressed with Donnie's reading comprehension and writing skills.

James looked up from his reading and quietly laughed to himself when he recalled a rare phone conversation he had with his son.

"Hey, how come you didn't tell me you were doing so well in your studies?" the Colonel had asked.

"Gee, Dad, it's all I do. How could I not do well?" Don didn't enjoy watching television much, and he wasn't currently involved in any sport, so his response seemed apropos.

The flight attendant's request for tray tables and seat backs to be placed in their upright position ended the reading session. He returned his carry-on to the seat in front and checked his watch, 11:30 PM Central Time. In just a few hours, James would be reunited with his mother and son.

……..

The Colonel had been looking forward to this moment for over a year. He pulled his truck onto Ellie's gravel driveway. Standing on the wraparound porch were his mother and now nearly 16-year-old son. Seeing Donnie standing on his own feet brought a smile to his face.

Ellie was standing next to the truck by the time her son opened the door. "Hello, Momma! How are things?"

"Much better now," replied Ellie hugging her son tightly.

"Careful, Momma, you might break something."

"It's just so good to see you, son," said Ellie wiping away a tear. Don stayed on the porch taking pictures of his only two family members.

"Hey, hot shot, you're looking good," said James, turning to Donnie.

"I'm getting there, Dad," answered Don while embracing his father.

"Show your dad the course, Donnie, while I fix lunch," suggested Mimi.

"Good idea, Mimi."

Father and son climbed into the gator with Donnie behind the wheel. "You're going to be impressed, Dad. The guys did a great job."

Don steered the vehicle to an area just south of Ellie's pond. As the course came into view, James whistled. "Wow, that IS impressive." Don parked the vehicle next to the pond while James looked over the course. "This reminds me of basic training."

The course consisted of a 30-foot long balance beam, a cargo net climb, a marine hurdle, weavers obstacle, 10-foot climbing wall, and a 20-yard sand pit which led to the 'Doozie,' the 140-yard hill with a 10- degree climb of 50 yards and a 15-degree decline of 90 yards. The hill was aptly named by Ellie the first time she saw it. The end of the hill was only 40 yards from the barn which still contained the climbing rope and punching bags. Dan had added an 84-hole peg board to the wall of the barn. The last additions were the four plyometric boxes. The shortest was 12 inches with the tallest being 36 inches.

"I can't wait to start using it. Rock said I could be fully cleared soon," said an antsy Don.

"Speaking of being cleared, when is your next appointment with Dr. Evans?"

"September 7th," answered Donnie quickly.

"That date sounds familiar; why would that be?" asked James, pretending not to know it was his son's 16th birthday.

"Ha, ha," said Don punching him in the arm.

"Do you think Mom has lunch ready?" asked James.

"Only one way to find out. Race ya to the gator," shouted Don as he broke into a sprint. To Don's amazement, his father caught him about 20 yards from the vehicle and was first to their destination. "Are you that fast, or am I that slow?" asked the winded 16-year-old.

"You've got to cut yourself some slack, son. You haven't run in over a year," his dad responded.

"I guess you're right," Don replied.

Then James added with a wink, "And the ole man still has a little juice in the tank."

When they reached the house, Donnie turned off the engine. He had been in deep thought during the short ride. "Dad, I've been pondering something for a long time."

"What's that, son?" James asked.

"My birthday is also the day Mom died. Is that hard for you?" asked Don.

After a momentary pause, James looked straight into Don's

eyes. "To be honest, Donnie, it's the other 364 days that are hard. September 7th is my day of *no regrets.*"

"Are you boys going to get out of the gator and eat, or what?" Ellie shouted from the screened door.

"Coming, Mimi."

Chapter 8

September 7th finally arrived. The Kelly boys headed for Wichita Falls for Donnie's appointment with Dr. Evans.

"Mimi says there is a girl in your life; is that true?" Don's face turned red at the question that seemed to come out of left field. James chuckled at Don's obvious discomfort. "What's her name? Where did you meet her? Is she pretty? Is she smart?" James asked in machine gun fashion.

"Her name is Cassamae Reynolds. I met her on a youth retreat in San Antonio last spring. She's tall, smart, and pretty. She lives in McKinney, plays volleyball, and is a 17-year-old junior. Her dad is a real estate broker, and her mom is a homemaker. Oh, and she has a brother who plays baseball at Dallas Baptist."

"Gee, Donnie, I didn't ask for a complete history," his dad quipped.

"I was just beating you to the punch, Dad. I know how 'detail-oriented' you are," said Don while making air quotes.

"What do you like best about her?"

Without hesitation Don responded. "She is who she says she is. You call it integrity, I think."

"How serious is this relationship?"

"Well, she's being recruited to play volleyball at Alabama," Don responded.

"Does she want to go there?"

"She was born in Tuscaloosa while her father was playing football for the Tide, so I think it's in her blood. I'm trying to develop a friendship because she's graduating a year before I am, and Alabama is too far to have a serious long distance relationship."

At that moment, the Colonel's phone rang "Yes sir.....okay, probably 3:30.....sounds great.....thank you sir, goodbye."

When the call ended, James went back to the conversation, "You came up with that by yourself?"

"Mimi and I talk a lot, Dad. It's nice to have a female perspective on things sometimes." Changing the subject, Don asked, "When do you have to go back overseas?"

"I report to Sheppard on the 28th and will return to duty October 1st," he answered, noticing Donnie's countenance change. "That means we have to make the days we have count" said James, rubbing Donnie's shoulder.

After receiving the news that Don was fully cleared, the Kellys grabbed burritos from the Burrito Shop and headed back to Van Alstyne.

"Heck of a way to celebrate your 16th birthday, isn't it?" asked the Colonel.

"It's not so bad. I got good news from the doctor, and I get to spend time alone with the Colonel."

"Speaking of being cleared, what's your plan?" asked James after finishing his last bite of his delicious burrito.

"I have been dying to work the course and get into shape. It's too late for football, but I hope to play baseball this year."

"You'll have to go to school on campus next semester," noted James.

"I've talked to Mrs. Seevers, and she says that should be no problem. She said I was ahead of the others and would benefit if I finished the semester at home. She also said that I could easily handle the dual credit courses offered by Grayson County College."

"I agree with her, son. Admit it, you're a nerd! Hey, I'll get you a pocket protector for your birthday."

"Real funny, Dad, real funny."

Returning to the plan, James asked, "Even after being broken up like you were, you still want to play football?"

"I'm a Kelly, Dad. I want to live my life and challenge my mind, body, and spirit. Being laid up for so long gave me a lot of time to read and reflect." After a short pause, Don continued, "You've always told me that God does not make us timid, but gives

40

us power, love and self-discipline."

The Colonel responded, "That's from 2nd Timothy. I haven't said that in a long time."

"I know I don't always appear to be listening, Dad, but I am. Besides, I feel like I've been cheated, and I don't want to waste my opportunities."

At that statement, James took out his wallet and handed it to Don. "Look inside and you'll find a folded index card. Take it out and read it."

Don found the frayed card behind his dad's driver's license. He opened it and read aloud, "Don't waste your opportunities."

"Is this the card you used to have on your mirror in high school?" Reading his father's surprise, Don confessed, "Mimi told me the story about Riley."

"That card has been a good reminder over the years. Riley was different. His outlook on life was one of a person who knew the final score would always be in his favor."

"Do you keep in touch with him?" asked Don, returning the card to the wallet.

"We call each other on our birthdays. I saw him about five years ago when I was in Memphis. He is a high school baseball coach just outside of the city."

"Is he still in a wheelchair?" asked Don.

"No, he does walk with a noticeable limp and uses a cane on occasion, but no chair."

Pondering his father's description of Riley, Donnie inquired, "What made him rare, dad?"

James checked his rearview mirrors, "You know why builders spend so much time on the foundation before they put up the walls?"

"So that the building will withstand the storms," replied Don confidently.

"That's right. Mr. and Mrs. Sprowl did a great job building

41

that foundation in him."

Don looked out the window and was tracing his facial scar with his index finger. Noticing, James asked, "What did Cassamae say about your scar?"

"Well, uh, at first nothing. I could tell she noticed and couldn't help but stare, so I just came out and told her what happened."

"That probably wasn't a good idea," suggested the elder Kelly.

"I think you're right. I was a little defensive with my attitude and embarrassed her a little. She quickly apologized for staring. I felt like a jerk and apologized for being so self-conscious."

"Has your Mimi met her?"

"Yes, when she picked me up after the retreat. One other time, Mimi, Cassie, and I did some work for the widow Tillett during the Great Days of Service in Van Alstyne."

"What does mom think about her?"

Don's reply came with a big smile. "She was impressed with her manners and work ethic. Mimi told me she liked that Cassie wasn't prissy and wasn't afraid to get dirty."

"I would like to meet her someday; she sounds like the real deal."

"Maybe someday, Dad."

As the Kelly boys pulled onto Ellie's driveway, Don noticed several cars. "What's going on at Mimi's?"

"You know Mimi; she wasn't going to let her only grandson have his 16th birthday without a party."

Looking at his father suspiciously, Don asked, "You knew this was going on? Why didn't you tell me?"

"I'm a Colonel in the United States Air Force. I'm trained not to give away classified information."

"Ha, ha," mocked Don.

By the time Don got out of the truck, everyone at the party

42

was standing on the porch. A loud "Happy Birthday" filled his ears. The Castle brothers, along with Vonda and Kay, stood next to Dan and Ellie. As Don reached the steps he hugged his Mimi. That's when he saw her—Cassamae Reynolds. "Happy birthday, Donnie," cooed Cassie.

Caught off guard by her presence and knowing all the adults were watching caused Don to hesitate, "Uh, thanks."

A voice behind asked, "Well, son aren't you going to introduce me to this pretty young lady?"

Regaining his composure, Donnie complied, "Cassamae Reynolds, this is my father Colonel James Kelly."

"Pleased to meet you sir," Cassie responded.

"Likewise," replied the Colonel. "Donnie says you are a volleyball player and a Crimson Tide fan."

"You know it," came her proud reply.

Well, this Ole Miss Rebel won't hold that against you," he said with a wink and a smile. Turning to Donnie, "Show Miss Cassie around the place while we get the food ready.

"Good idea, Dad. Hop in the Gator, Cassie, and I'll give you a tour." Spending time with Cassie was pure joy for Don. Her sense of humor was infectious, and he appreciated her quick wit. She was well versed in a plethora of topics which kept silence at bay. They both liked to read and even had a common favorite author, Vince Flynn. Donnie was surprised to hear that she liked black ops type novels. Cassie told him her father brought one of his novels on vacation and after reading it, she was hooked.

After the dinner, cake, and gift opening, Don walked Miss Reynolds to her car. "Thank you for being here. I really enjoyed talking with you, Cassie."

"Me too, Donnie. I know you don't do social network stuff, but it's okay if you call me. I'm really busy with school and volleyball, but I would like to hear from you once in awhile."

"That sounds good," said Don while opening the door to her red Ford Taurus, letting her slip inside.

Don stood watching her disappear, thinking about how much he had enjoyed his 16th birthday.

Chapter 9

On the night before Colonel Kelly was to return to Sheppard Air Force Base, Don was awakened by a loud clap of thunder. The late September storm pounded the roof. He looked at the clock beside his bed which read 12:28. After using the bathroom, he realized the lights were on downstairs.

As he descended the stairs, he saw his father and Mimi sitting at the dining room table. In front of Ellie was a Kleenex box with a pile of used tissues next to it. She was dabbing her eyes when she noticed her grandson at the bottom of the stairs. "What's wrong, Mimi?" Ellie unsuccessfully tried to hide her emotions.

Noticing his mother's embarrassment, James took over. "Come here, son, and we'll get you up to speed." Don sat down between his remaining family members. He looked at his father with guarded anticipation. "Your Mimi has cancer son."

The words hit Donnie with hammer-like force. His eyes filled with tears as he turned to his dear grandmother. "You're going to be okay, aren't you, Mimi?" asked Don, sounding more hopeful than convinced.

Over the next hour he learned that his grandmother had stage four breast cancer. During a routine physical, a lump was found, and further tests revealed the cancer had metastasized to her lungs. He also learned that Ellie refused chemo and radiation. She had agreed to any experimental treatments that might become available. When Donnie asked why she wouldn't do chemo or radiation, she simply said, "Donnie, I just don't believe the side effects are worth it." The doctors couldn't tell Ellie how long she had on this earth, with the prognosis being anywhere from a few months to a year.

They all agreed that Donnie would keep taking his classes off campus. Ellie did not want Don to miss another year of athletics and voiced her opinion. She gave in when Donnie said, "Before Grandpa Floyd gets you back, I want to spend as much time with you as I can."

The Colonel was going to have to be overseas for a minimum of six months. The conflict was escalating, and his men needed his leadership.

By 2 A.M. the storm had passed. After praying for God's direction and peace, the Kelly's retired to their rooms.

The next eight months saw Ellie's health decline. Despite her high pain threshold and incredible will, the cancer was taking its toll. She was sleeping longer and more often. When she was awake, she tried valiantly to do her daily routine. Her morning always started with her "quiet time," which included reading the Bible and praying. She would fix breakfast for herself and her grandson every morning. After washing the dishes, Ellie would make her bed, grab her current novel and read. On nice days, she would read while sitting on her porch swing.

Her favorite diversion was when she would ride the Gator down to the pond to watch Donnie running the obstacle course in the late afternoon. Her grandson worked the course six days a week.

On most days, the young Kelly would throw baseballs and footballs at various targets he set up on the property. His father taught him how to punt and kick at an early age. Donnie found that kicking footballs relieved a lot of the stress he had over his grandmother's health. The best stress relievers, however, were the punching bags in the barn. Don would punch the bags to exhaustion —and sometimes, tears.

Watching his dying grandmother live her faith had a great impact on Don, deepening his understanding of the applicable nature of the Bible.

The month of June was bittersweet for the Kellys. The Colonel was home from his assignment in the Middle East. Having all three of them together was enjoyable, but they realized their time together must be short. James and Don would fish and work the course when Ellie was resting. Donnie, now 6'2 and 190 pounds, had regained his strength and speed. Playing catch was something the

Kelly men cherished the most. It brought back memories of the days before the accident.

When Ellie was unable to move around, the men would cook the meals and spend time with their dying loved one. On cooler nights, they would sit on the porch swing and talk. It was becoming apparent Ellie was nearing the time when sitting on the porch swing would be a thing of the past.

On one late June night, Ellie told the boys she wanted to be buried in Clarksdale, Mississippi, next to Floyd. She had purchased the plot the week she learned of her cancer.

"Don," said the Colonel.

"Sir?" came the reply.

"Mimi and I have been talking and think it would be a good idea to emancipate you. With Mimi's health and the situation overseas, we think it would be best to make you a legal adult."

"What exactly does that do, Dad?"

"Well, you know how to take care of yourself, so we don't see a need for a guardian." James continued, "You've been paying the bills and are very handy around the house. Heck, Donnie, you've been an adult for a long time."

Ellie added, "I have some money saved, and this week your dad and I are going to put your name on the account. I will also be signing over everything I have to you."

The weight of the new information overwhelmed young Kelly. All he could do was watch the dance of the fireflies as he became immersed in his thoughts.

Chapter 10

It was August 22nd. Donnie woke up to his alarm at 5:30 AM. He grabbed his Bible off the nightstand and headed downstairs. Don set the book on the edge of the table and went to the refrigerator for some orange juice. Upon his return, he bumped the table and his Bible fell to the floor. When he picked it up he noticed it was open to Psalm 103. Verses 15-18 were highlighted. "As for man, his days are like grass; as a flower of the field, so he flourishes. When the wind has passed over it, it is no more, and its place acknowledges it no longer."

A chill came over Don, and he stopped reading. An audible "Mimi" came from his lips. He turned and looked at her closed door. Donnie set the Bible back on the table and slowly walked to his grandmother's room. As he placed his hand on the knob, he could feel his pulse. The adrenaline was raging in his body causing his hand to shake.

Don took a deep breath and opened the door. Ellie was on her back with her mouth open. With much trepidation, he went to her bedside. Tears started streaming down his face as he realized his Mimi was gone. He closed her mouth and kissed her on her forehead. His shoulders started to shake as the tears turned to uncontrollable sobbing. The broken young man dropped to his knees beside the bed with his face buried and his hand on his grandmother's lifeless body.

When he regained his composure, Donnie got up from his kneeling position to call his father in Wichita Falls.

Honoring his mother's request, a week later James and Don stood by Ellie's gravesite situated near her beloved husband. Pastor Henderson, now in his eighties, performed the graveside service. It was a hot and muggy late August day in Clarksdale, Mississippi. The beauty of the setting sun caught Don's attention. "Hey, Dad, look at that sunset."

James turned and gazed at the horizon. After several seconds of drinking in God's glory, he said, "On the day we buried your grandfather, there was thunder, lightning, and rain. That storm was exactly what was going on inside me at the time. I find it ironic that this gorgeous sunset epitomizes how I feel today. Your Mimi has looked so forward to being with your grandfather, that I actually have a part of me that sees the beauty of that reunion."

As they walked to the car, the burial crew passed them on the way to place their beloved Ellie in the ground. A black F150 was parked nose to nose to James' rental car. Standing beside the vehicle was a bearded man in a dark suit. "It can't be," whispered James.

"Can't be who, Dad?"

By the time they reached the vehicles, the man had removed his sunglasses revealing his identity. Without saying a word, the two men briefly embraced. "Donnie, I'd like to introduce you to Riley Joe Sprowl." Riley and Don shook hands,

"Nice grip. Jimmy, you've got a good looking boy here."

"Even with this scar?" asked Don while pointing to his injury.

Riley retorted, "Are you kidding? Haven't you ever heard the saying, 'Chicks dig scars'?"

Don glanced at his father. "Dad says that all the time."

"Well, your dad's a smart guy," Riley said laughing. Changing the subject, Riley continued, "I'm sorry about your mother, Jimmy. She was a terrific person."

James nodded in appreciation and said, "You're looking well. How are you doing these days?"

"Still have to use this," pointing to his cane, "but all in all, I'm a blessed man. When are you headed back to the Lone Star State?" asked RJ.

"We are planning on heading back tomorrow. We've got a room at the Holiday Inn in town."

"Great, how about I buy you guys dinner at the Rib Shack, so we can catch up, and I can get to know ole Donnie boy here."

James looked at his son who nodded in the affirmative.

"Sounds great."

Riley and the Kelly boys spent the next two and a half hours talking about everything from their high school days to the present. Donnie could see why Riley Joe meant so much to his dad. He was a great storyteller with a clever sense of humor. An additional perk for Don was the new information he learned about his father. According to Riley, James Kelly was one of the best athletes to come out of Clarksdale. The most intriguing revelation was learned while the Colonel was away phoning the base.

"Donnie, did your dad ever tell you about him saving two lives?" asked RJ.

"No sir. He never has."

"I'm not surprised. Your dad never talked much about himself, even though he had a lot to talk about."

"Please tell me" encouraged Don.

"Love to" replied Riley. "One night after my accident, we were coming home in my parents' van. We were the first to come upon a two car accident on Highway 61. One of the cars was upside down and on fire. Before I knew it, your dad was out of the van racing toward the burning car. I watched him pull a man out of the driver's seat through the door that came open during the crash. He used a fireman's carry to get him out of harm's way. The amazing thing was that the unconscious man weighed at least forty pounds more than your dad.

"After Jimmy got the man to safety, he returned to the car. The fire was accelerating, but your dad didn't seem to notice. He was on all fours looking into the back of the vehicle. The next thing I knew, your dad disappeared into the car through a broken window." Don was looking at Riley with his eyes and mouth wide open. "My heart was pounding as I watched the fire grow with Jimmy still in the car. Finally, I saw his feet as he backed out of the car. In his arms was a small boy. He carried the boy to the side of the father who was still unconscious. A woman pulled up, and your dad directed her get

50

help. Remember, Donnie, there were no cell phones back then.

"Finally, Jimmy went to the other vehicle which was on the other side of the road. The bed of the truck was in a ditch with the front facing upward with one headlight still on. The man was conscious but, according to your dad, obviously drunk.

"The emergency vehicles arrived and took over the situation. One of them noticed your dad had a very bloody shirt. Apparently, he had a pretty severe laceration just below his ribs. He ended up having twelve stitches. The most amazing thing, Donnie, was that during the whole ordeal, your dad was as cool as a cucumber."

"So that's how Dad got that scar," said Don. "I asked him about it, and all he said was that he cut himself on broken glass."

"Ole James has been like that since I've known him, son."

Colonel Kelly came into Riley's line of sight, so he stopped talking. He tapped Don on the hand and slightly shook his head no.

"Only believe half of what you hear with this guy, Donnie boy. He's got a great imagination," lectured the Colonel as he returned to his seat.

"He does tell a great story; I'll give him that," added Don.

Before James could respond, Riley interjected, "Well boys, I've got to be getting back home before the Mrs. sends out a posse."

"Thanks for the dinner, Mr. Sprowl."

"Call me RJ, Donnie. All my friends do."

"Yes sir, Mr. RJ."

Riley looked at James who responded with a shrug of his shoulders. "You military families. Always polite and formal. Gotta admit, I like it."

As the Kellys watched their friend drive away, James said matter-of-factly, "That's a great man, son."

"Like you always say, Dad, iron sharpens iron."

On the flight home, James and Don finished their conversation about their next move. The Colonel informed his son that he had one more tour overseas and was contemplating

51

retirement upon his return. They agreed that Don would live in Van Alstyne and start taking classes on campus second semester.

"You don't have anything keeping you from playing baseball next semester Donnie."

"I haven't played since eighth grade, Dad. I'm a junior now."

"You'll find it's like riding a bike, son. Besides, I've watched you throwing the baseball at your targets and am amazed how strong and accurate you are."

"I've got to admit, I sure do miss competing," said Don reflectively.

"It's in your blood, son. I look forward to watching you play again. I've missed that part of our lives myself. Okay, let's go over the plan one more time," said the Colonel changing the subject.

"I'll drive Mimi's truck for transportation and pay the bills from the checking account we set up. The $25,000 Mimi left will be in the account plus the money you send me monthly. I'm responsible for the upkeep of the property. I'll cut wood and give it away to needy families for my community service. I'll be spending half of my school day taking courses at Grayson Community College, so I can get a jump on college. I'm going to try out for the baseball team in the spring. Oh, and if I need someone, the Castle brothers are there for me."

"Sounds like you've got it down," said the confident father. Looking into his son's eyes, the Colonel confessed, "Don, I'm sorry you have to grow up so fast, but life happens and you never know where it will lead. I trust and believe in you. And, of course, I'll be praying for you every day."

Chapter 11

Baseball tryouts were finally here. Don had spent the last four months marking out the calendar leading up to this day. It was his third week of being on campus. Don's quiet personality and his taking college courses in the morning didn't afford him many opportunities to make friends. The small school atmosphere did draw attention to the *new kid*. His facial scar also drew some attention which no longer fazed the young Kelly.

The tryouts were at the ballpark about two miles from the campus. There were 45 players competing for the 32 slots available to be divided between the Junior Varsity and Varsity teams. The first day of the 3-day tryout found threatening skies with a temperature of 56 degrees. After Coach Jimmy Haynes welcomed the participants, he divided the players into three groups. There were 10 returning varsity, 12 returning JV, and 23 new players, of which 11 were freshmen.

The returning Varsity players were sent to the batting cages with Coach Taylor Penn. The JV went with Coach Scott Ritchie to run the 60 yard dash. Coach Haynes watched the "newbies" throwing mechanics and arm strength while they threw long toss. It didn't take long for Coach Haynes to spot Donnie's throwing skills. "What's your name, son?"

"Don Kelly, sir."

"I haven't seen you on campus. Did you just move here?"

"No, sir, I've lived in Van Alstyne for three years, but I was schooled at home because of an injury."

"What year in school are you?" asked Haynes.

"I'm a junior, but I haven't played since I was an eighth grader."

About that time a bolt of lightning struck followed close by a loud clap of thunder. "Everyone in the clubhouse!" yelled Coach Haynes. The 45 players scurried to the clubhouse, grabbing their personal equipment on the way.

Once inside, Coach Penn checked a weather app on his cell phone. "There's a line of storms headed our way. We've got about 20 minutes or so."

"Okay guys, those of you with cars need to leave. If your parents aren't here, call them now," ordered the seasoned head coach.

Within minutes the clubhouse was nearly empty. Don was nearing his truck when he saw a freshman on the phone. "Need a ride?" asked Don.

"Yes, my parents are in Plano."

"Hop in," ordered Don.

By the time Don dropped him off, the first storm hit. Hail was mixed in the heavy rain and there were straight line winds of 50-plus miles per hour. The young Kelly was white knuckling the steering wheel while quietly praying for protection. As the visibility worsened, Donnie's focus on the car in front of him increased. Suddenly the car disappeared.

Seconds later Don found out the reason for the disappearance. The bridge had partially collapsed, leaving the driver nowhere to go except into the water. Donnie's slow speed allowed him enough time to stop before finding himself in the same predicament.

He turned on his emergency flashers and ran to the edge of what remained of the bridge. The white Nissan was in the rushing water on its driver's side with the lights still on. With his adrenaline pumping, Don ran back to his truck, grabbed his bat, and a flashlight from the glove box. He ran down the bank upriver of the Nissan. Without hesitation he jumped into the freezing water and allowed the current to take him to the vehicle.

He climbed onto the car which was two-thirds covered with water. The flashlight revealed a woman's face staring back at him. Her eyes were exceptionally wide with little emotion behind them. Don surmised she was in some level of shock.

"Cover your head," Don yelled, while also giving her visual

directions. After the third time, the frightened woman responded. She covered her head and upper torso with her jacket. Don used his bat to break the front passenger side window. He cleared the remaining jagged edges the best he could. With the hard rain continuing to fall, Don tossed his bat onto the bridge and reached for the woman. She grabbed his arm with a grip fueled by fear. Just as Don cleared the petite female from the window, the Nissan shifted, causing him to lose his balance. He instinctively gave her a bear hug as he fell backwards into the water hitting his head and torso on a sizable chunk of the collapsed bridge.

As painful as the fall was, it kept Donnie and his charge from fully falling into the water. The pair pulled themselves up to higher ground eventually reaching the road. Seeing the Nissan on its roof, lights still on, with only the tires partially showing, prompted the grateful survivor to hug Don. "God bless you," were the only words she was able to muster before losing herself to uncontrollable sobbing.

"Are you two alright?" came a voice from the other side of the bridge. "I called 911. They should be here any minute."

As Donnie lifted his right arm to wave, excruciating pain indicated he was not all right. When the paramedics arrived, Don walked the shaken woman to them and then returned to his truck, after retrieving his bat from the bridge. Trying to ignore the pain, Don called the Castle brothers for help.

Within minutes, Bill and Argie arrived on the scene. Argie jumped into the driver's seat while Donnie slid over. They dropped off Don's truck and drove him to Wilson N. Jones Hospital in Sherman.

The x-rays revealed two breaks in the humerus. The arm had to be casted in a way that would prevent Don from driving his Mimi's standard transmission truck.

The storms had ended by the time Don and the Castle brothers left the hospital. As Bill drove his passenger to his home, he noticed Donnie's dejected countenance. "What's on your mind son?"

"I was so excited to finally get to play baseball again and this happens," pointing to his casted arm. "If this is God's plan for me, I've got to say, it sucks."

Bill glanced over at his passenger, "Don, could it have been God's plan to use you tonight to save someone's life?" Without letting the boy answer, Bill continued, "Yes, it cost you a broken arm and another year without baseball, but, the more important question is—was it worth it?"

"OUCH. You don't mince words, do you?" said Don through a sheepish grin.

Chapter 12

The cast came off at the beginning of March, which allowed Don to resume self-sufficiency. Vonda and Kay Castle took turns cooking and cleaning for Don while he was incapacitated.

He, once again, returned to working with Mrs. Seevers while being homebound. One positive for Don was the news that he had earned a 35 on the ACT.

Another perk was working with Rock King again. Don and Rock had developed a bond during his long, arduous rehabilitation from the truck accident. Don enjoyed the varied topics of discussion the two of them had during their work. Young Kelly could sense that Mr. King knew exactly what he needed with his father so far away.

Once Don was able to drive, he and Cassie went out on occasion. They had become good friends over the last two years. He watched her lead the Lady Lions to the State Semi-Finals before being knocked out of the tournament. Cassie accepted a full scholarship offer from Alabama, which had been her dream.

Even though his affection for Cassamae Reynolds was growing, he had to face the reality of their being apart his senior year. Donnie longed for his Mimi's wisdom during these times.

In late June, Colonel Kelly returned from overseas on a surprise visit. The Kelly boys spent two weeks watching baseball. Their first stop was the College World Series in Omaha, Nebraska. On the way home, they attended Major League games in Kansas City and St. Louis.

The last leg of the journey was in Arlington, where they watched the Rangers play the Yankees. Having his father to talk to for two straight weeks did wonders for the young man. As they pulled onto the driveway, Donnie couldn't help but think of how much better he felt when his father was around.

The last two weeks of the Colonel's leave was spent fixing up the property, working the obstacle course, and playing catch like the old days. They also renewed their tradition of fishing the pond.

On July 4th, with a lantern providing the only light on a moonless night, James and Don sat in their chairs with their fishing lines still in the water. Donnie broke the silence, "Dad, why do you serve? Is it because you like to fly?"

"No, son. I love this country with all my heart. I feel blessed to be born here."

"But, Dad, if you listen to people on TV, in Hollywood, or even some politicians, you would think the U.S. is an uncaring place, full of arrogant people."

Shaking his head in agreement, the Colonel said, "I know, Donnie, but the founding of America was probably the most successful experiment of all time. Even with all her flaws, this country is, as it has been called, 'A beacon on a hill.' "

Don asked, "I get why people from other countries may not like us, but why do so many, who live here, hate it so much? Why don't they just leave, if it is so bad?"

"That's a valid question, son. Abraham Lincoln said that the destruction of this country will come from within—a kind of national suicide. Some people assuage their guilt for living in such a prosperous nation by trashing the provider of that prosperity."

James grabbed his pole and reeled in his line. "This country has truly been blessed, and I serve in appreciation of that blessing."

The first wave of fireworks burst overhead. James turned off the lantern while they returned to silence watching the patriotic display.

The uniformed Colonel threw his bag in the back of his truck early the next morning. His thirty day leave had flown by. James always struggled with leaving his son. It became even more difficult since Ellie's death. He partially opened his door, looking at Don standing on the porch.

"See you in December, Donnie boy. I love you."

"Love you too, Dad." James headed down the gravel driveway looking in the rearview mirror at his son still standing on the porch with his hands in his pockets.

Feeling overwhelmed with emotion, the Colonel stopped his truck and got out. He yelled back at Don, "Don Floyd Kelly, you are the most courageous person I know. I'm proud to call you my son."

The younger Kelly tapped his chest twice and pointed at his father. The Colonel waved and got back into the truck and looked into the mirror one more time. "Lord, please watch over my boy."

Chapter 13

"Sorry I'm late, guys," apologized Coach Jack Wylie, as he joined the other Van Alstyne Panther football coaches for their last preseason meeting. "I think I may have found what we are looking for."

"How so?" asked Coach Mike Miller.

"I was accidentally on County Road 619 and out of nowhere a football hits right in front of my truck. I slammed on my brakes and got out. A kid was jogging my way. Coach, he was at least forty yards away."

"Did he throw it at your truck?" asked Taylor Penn.

Jack took the floor again, "No, he punted the ball. When he reached me, he was apologizing all over the place. When he told me what happened, I asked him to punt it back where he came from. He booted it over 50 yards with over a 4 second hang time." The coaches looked at each other with skepticism. "That's why I'm late. I watched him punt and kick for ten minutes. This kid is the real deal, Coach Miller."

Wylie's excitement was hard to contain. "He's got an interesting story: he's a senior, lives alone, and has never played football. His father is an Air Force pilot. Oh, and he's 6'2" and weighs close to 200, a real specimen. I asked him why I never saw him on campus and he said he was badly injured in a car wreck when he was a freshman. He said he has been schooled at home."

"Does he have a scar on his face?" asked Coach Haynes.

"From here to here," replied Jack outlining Don's scar.

"Hey, that's the kid from baseball tryouts," noted Coach Penn.

"Don Kelly," added Jimmy Haynes.

"Yep, that's the guy," confirmed Wylie. "He said he'll be here tomorrow. By the way, you should see his set up. It's an obstacle course that is military worthy. Kelly says he works it six days a week. This kid seems really *old school*."

Texas High School Football was more than just a sport. There were 90 young men wearing blue with PANTHERS written in white across the chest. Their white helmets glistened in the early morning August sun.

There were high expectations for the upcoming season. The Panthers were solid on both sides of the ball, with their only weaknesses being the kicking game and depth in the defensive secondary.

The obvious perceived leader was Paul Gunn, a 6'4"/250-pound senior middle linebacker who also played fullback on occasion. Gunn was very talented and was being recruited by most of the Big 12 Conference schools. He was brash and arrogant, having no problem speaking his mind. His love for weightlifting was demonstrated by his muscular frame and his name on the top of the record boards in the weight room.

The coaches positioned the seniors and juniors on one sideline and the freshmen and sophomores on the other for stretching and agilities. The mandatory four days in shorts and helmets were used for conditioning and implementation of the offense and defense. Don Kelly would be spending most of his time kicking footballs.

After wearing pads for several days in the Texas heat, the Panthers looked forward to competing against someone different. Saturday's scrimmage versus neighboring Gunter High was just what the doctor ordered.

Don stood on the sidelines during the controlled portion of the scrimmage. During the 12 minute quarter ending the competition, Don punted twice with no defensive pressure, averaging 39 yards per punt.

The following week, the Panthers travelled to Gainesville for their second scrimmage. The Leopards were one class larger than the 3A Panthers and provided stiffer competition. VA struggled moving the ball on offense and also had trouble stopping Gainesville. Don punted 3 times for an impressive average of 43 yards per punt.

There was considerable grumbling on the bus ride home that escalated inside the locker room. Paul Gunn slammed his helmet on top of his locker yelling, "Listen up!" Immediately the room went silent. "I'm working my butt off out there and some of you are playing like a bunch of pansies."

Gunn caught Don's eye, "What are you looking at, Scarface?" The room was silent, with all eyes focused on the confrontation. Don didn't respond, nor did he redirect his eyes. Gunn kept his threatening glare and said, "You're just a kicker. You're not really a football player, so you can go home now." Without any change in his expression, Don calmly retrieved his possessions and left.

Monday's practice brought its own excitement. It was the first day of school and the week of the first game. It was also the second Monday of TGW, which was the acronym for Tough Guys Win. The man vs. man competition separated the men from the boys.

The week before, Paul Gunn won the BELT by being the most dominant competitor. The BELT was a replica of a WWE Belt, which would hang in the winner's locker for the week. The winner could not challenge anyone, but could be challenged. No one expected Gunn to be challenged for the remainder of the year.

The players circled the school emblem in the middle of the sports turf field. "Who's first to challenge someone?" asked Coach Miller. Starting running back, Travis Williams challenged starting outside linebacker Jim Gatto. The two good friends loved competing against each other. Their trash talking stopped on Miller's whistle. They came out of their stances and collided like two rams trying to establish dominance. Their raucous teammates cheered the battle which was won by Williams.

"Now, that's football," crowed offensive line coach, Dru Murray. Gatto and Williams tapped each other on the helmet and returned to the circle.

After several challenges, Miller called for one more. A voice came from just outside the circle, "I want to challenge Paul Gunn." Silence fell over the group.

"Who has a death wish?" taunted Gunn looking around for the culprit. Don stepped into the circle, "That would be me."

"Are you freaking kidding me—the kicker?" said the linebacker in disbelief.

Gunn joined Don in the circle seething, "Let's go, pal. I'm going to teach you a lesson you'll never forget." Don buckled his chin strap and positioned himself in the middle of the emblem. Paul placed his face mask on Don's and said through clinched teeth, "Big mistake, Kelly, big mistake."

Don smiled and put in his mouth piece. The other players and coaches were eerily quiet. The two combatants each got in a three point stance with their masks about a foot apart.

"On my whistle," directed the head coach. When the whistle blast sounded, Donnie shot toward his opponent with incredible quickness. He got underneath Gunn's shoulder pads while driving his legs, lifting the surprised 250 pounder up and onto his back with Kelly landing on top of him. Don lifted his head and smashed his face mask into that of his prone foe. Without saying a word, Don stood up and walked away.

The stunned players and coaches looked around before letting out a collective roar at seeing Goliath fall.

Standing next to his boss, Coach Wylie leaned in, "We might have more than a kicker here."

"I believe no truer words have been spoken," replied the smiling mentor.

After what was easily the most energetic practice of the early season, Don was asked to stay on the field while the other players headed for the showers. "Are you sure you haven't played football before?" asked Miller. "I've never seen what I saw today."

"My father was a football player at Ole Miss and has taught me a lot about strength, speed, and leverage."

"Well, son, you learned well, that's for sure." Coach Miller continued, "Are you interested in playing any other positions?"

"Yes, sir."

"We are a little thin in the secondary," informed Michael.

"My dad was a safety. He loved the strategy of trying to stop the other team. We would talk about it all the time while fishing."

"Well, Mr. Kelly, starting tomorrow we'll see if you picked anything up from those conversations."

The noisy locker room fell silent when Don walked through the door. Gunn walked toward Donnie with his hands behind his back. The look on his face was less than friendly. Donnie dropped his helmet on the floor preparing for his second confrontation of the day. The massive linebacker stopped inches from his adversary. "Kelly, you kicked my butt; this belongs to you," turning over the belt he held behind his back.

Don let out the breath he had been holding and took the belt. Gunn turned to the surrounding players, "Gentlemen, let me introduce you to our newest tough guy, Don Kelly. Ready? Clap." The players clapped 3 times in unison, as per tradition.

"Hey, Kelly, we're going to Romano's for pizza. Do you want to go?" asked quarterback Armando Avina.

Don took his hand off his door handle and turned around to see Avina, Gunn, and center Mike James, waiting for his answer. "Sure."

"Ride with me," ordered Paul pointing at his black Range Rover. "Williams and Gatto are meeting us there."

The six seniors devoured four large pizzas while making fun of each other. Gunn took the brunt of the abuse for getting whipped by the kicker. Don watched his other teammates enjoying each other's company and realized he hadn't experienced this type of camaraderie since his move to Texas. The other five players had been together since kindergarten and had a brotherly bond. Donnie had spent so much time alone; he had not realized what he was

64

missing.

"So, Kelly, what's your story?" asked Avina. Donnie looked at the five sets of eyes looking at him with anticipation, and decided to be transparent with his new friends.

For the next several minutes, Donnie shared his version of his life starting with the loss of his mother at birth to the present day. The young men were enthralled by their new teammate's story.

"Dude, how come you aren't an angry jerk?" spouted Travis.

"My dad has taught me that when you have negative circumstances, you either overcome them or they overcome you. Besides, I've got a friend in Jesus," smiled Don.

"You sound like a preacher," noted Armando.

"Does this mean I'm out of the group?" inquired Donnie.

"Hell, I mean, heck no," said Paul laughing. "This is the Bible Belt, and we all hear about that at church. Your living it out in real life is impressive; that's all." The others shook their heads in agreement. "In fact," Gunn continued, "I'm so inspired, I'm buying."

Chapter 14

"Hey Cassie, this is Don."

"Hi, Donnie. I'm sorry I didn't return your call. I've been really busy with volleyball and school."

"No problem, Cass. I just wanted to let you know I was playing football."

"That's great. I know how frustrated you've been with all the things keeping you from playing. I'm really happy for you." Cassamae continued, "We are playing A&M next Friday. It's going to be televised on ESPN 2. I've been getting a lot of playing time, so watch if you can."

"I'll record it," promised Don.

"So, are you dating anyone Donnie?"

"Me? No, don't you know I'm interested in a girl in Alabama?" said Don laughing.

After a short pause, "Donnie, I've got another call, could you hold for a second?" Cassie covered the receiver and waited several seconds before continuing their conversation. "I'm sorry Donnie, I've got to go. Good luck with football."

Somewhat taken off guard, Don stammered, "Oh, okay Cass, I'll talk to you later."

"Bye Donnie."

….

Friday night had finally arrived. Don Kelly would be playing his first football game two weeks shy of his 18th birthday. The home game against Ford High was highly anticipated. They were picked to win their district and looked to be a formidable opponent. In fact, all three preseason opponents were highly touted.

Don was in the team room watching video from Ford's scrimmages. He had practiced two days at safety and wasn't expecting to play. However, his father had always said that "Proper preparedness prevents piss poor performance." The younger Kelly trusted and admired his father and figured his advice was worth

66

adherence.

Don wanted to share this new experience with his father, but he had not received any direct communication from him in the last month. The only contact came from an airman from Sheppard who told him his father would call when his latest mission was over.

Paul Gunn helped Donnie pull on his number 8 jersey over his pads. "Are you nervous, big shooter?"

"Not really, Paul. In fact, I'm so happy to finally be able to put this uniform on, I want to cry."

"Don't do that, for Pete's sake."

"Don't worry. I know there's no crying in football," said Don while punching the padded linebacker.

Paul placed his hand on Donnie's shoulder pad and looked him square in the eyes. "Thank you Kelly."

"For what?"

"For teaching me a valuable lesson. No one has ever put me in my place like you did. You made me realize I've been nothing but an a-hole my whole life."

"Amen," came a voice behind Gunn.

Paul turned around to see Armando and Travis. "Kelly, because of you, we actually can stand being around this narcissist for longer periods of time," chirped Williams.

"Now, can we stop this touchy-feely stuff and play some football?" quipped Avina.

The adrenaline surged through Kelly's body as the team ran out of the blow up tunnel led by two 'Blue Crew' members carrying the American and Texas flags. The student body and parents extended the tunnel screaming for their boys, while the band played the school's fight song.

"So this is Friday Night Lights in Texas," thought Donnie as he absorbed the moment.

The teams were very evenly matched and were tied 14-14 at the half. Don punted 3 times for a 44-yard average. Starting safety

Robert Randall intercepted a pass in the Panther's end zone on the last play of the first half to keep the score deadlocked.

Don's kick to start the second half was fielded on the one yard line. The speedy returner broke through the Panther kick off team, dubbed the "hammerheads," and was headed for an apparent 99-yard touchdown until he was met by the kicker at the 50 yard line. The force of the blow ejected the ball from the carrier, along with his helmet and chin strap. Van Alstyne's photographer, Griff Servati, caught all three objects flying in separate directions. The photo made it in 3 different North Texas newspapers the next day.

The crowd erupted in a combination of gasps and cheers. Before Don reached his sideline, he was met by special teams coach Jaycee Guerrero, who nearly knocked his kicker over with a chest bump.

On the very next play, Avina hit his favorite receiver, Nick Nobriga, for a 47-yard touchdown pass. The Panthers took advantage of the momentum shift, scoring two more times: Williams on a 9-yard run and Donnie with a 40-yard field goal. Gunn led the defense with 12 tackles and 2 QB sacks. Randall ended the game with his second interception. The 31-14 victory was a positive start to the season.

Chapter 15

Donnie invited Nobriga, Gunn, and Avina for a barbecue on Saturday. It was the first time he had anyone from the team over.

"Dude, this place is sweet," stated Paul emphatically, while looking over the obstacle course.

"You live here by yourself?" asked Nick.

"I do when my Dad is overseas."

"Have you had any parties?"

"Yeah, this one," responded Don with a laugh. "Let's eat and watch my girl on TV."

"You have a girlfriend?" asked a surprised Avina.

"She's not really my girl; she's just the only girl I've talked to. Her name is Cassie. She plays volleyball for Alabama."

Don started the recorded game from the night before.

"Which one is she, Kelly?" asked Paul.

From the kitchen Don yelled, "She's number 10."

The guys stared intently at the screen looking for Miss Cassie. "There she is," said Armando. "She's in the front row."

"She's a hottie, Kelly. And looks good in spandex, I might add," commented Paul, drawing a head shake from Nobriga.

Donnie and his new friends ate, laughed, and watched the match over the next hour, which was won by Alabama in three games.

While Don was taking dirty dishes to the kitchen, Nick noticed something on the TV. The ESPN commentator was interviewing the Alabama coach with several players in the background.

"Hey, isn't that Cassie in the back with that guy? Paul and Armando joined Nick.

"Do you think that's her boyfriend?" whispered Armando.

An instant later, the guy kissed and hugged Cassie. "Pause it," ordered Gunn. Nick grabbed the remote and paused the recording. "Do you know who that guy is?" asked Paul rhetorically.

69

"That's the Crimson Tide quarterback, Curt Burns."

"Why are you guys whispering?"

All three startled players whipped around to see Donnie looking at the frozen screen. He did his best to hide his embarrassment.

The uncomfortable silence was broken by Paul, "Hey, I've got to go. If you two want a ride, the train is leaving."

"See you Monday, Kelly," said Avina, as he and the others hurried out the door.

When the guys were safely out of earshot, Nick half whispered, "That was rough. That kid has no luck."

"Oh, he has luck; it's just all bad," suggested Armando as he climbed into Gunn's Range Rover.

Donnie stared at the screen for several seconds before he grabbed the remote and pressed *delete.*

....Anna, Texas

The Anna Coyotes were the next opponent for the Panthers. Anna was coming off their best season in years, returning nine defensive starters.

After the short five-mile ride, the players stepped off the bus to see a nearly packed stadium. The year before, the 4A Coyotes defeated the 3A Panthers handily, which prompted the coaching staff to try to find some kind of motivational edge; so they decided to do the pregame at home and show up near game time.

The favored Coyotes scored on their first possession of the game. Robert Randall returned the ensuing kickoff to the fifty, but Avina's first pass was picked off and run back for a touchdown. By half time, VA found themselves behind 28-0. The only positive, was the 48-yard average on Don's five punts.

Rock King came out of the visitors' locker room and approached the coaches who were huddled outside. "Randall is out."

All of the coaches turned in unison toward Rock. "When did he get hurt?" asked a surprised Coach Haynes.

Rock answered, "I'm pretty sure he is having major appendix problems. He is throwing up and was very tender in that area. Matt Braddock is going to get his parents to take him to the hospital."

"Who is his backup?" asked Miller.

"Kelly" answered Coach Guerrero.

"Well, I guess we will get to see what the kid's got," stated Jack Wylie.

A dispirited mood met the coaches as they entered the room for the halftime adjustments. The well respected Randall was an integral part of the team.

After coordinators Justin Dozier and Wylie made their adjustments, Coach Miller gathered the team. "Men, you can't re-saw sawdust. What matters now is how we respond. Let's go."

Don Kelly stood next to Travis Williams on the ten yard line waiting for the second half kickoff. "Hey number 8." Don turned toward Williams. "They are going to kick it to you, so let's take it to the house; I'll lead the way."

Donnie took a deep breath, trying to control the adrenaline surge. As predicted, the kick went to the rookie returner who received it on the five yard line. Travis ran in front of him yelling, "Let's go."

The two returners made it to the wall set up by the return team. The only Coyote making it through the wall was dispatched by Williams, allowing Don to run by the prone opponent on his way to the end zone.

"Now that's what I'm talking about," exclaimed Travis while smacking the top of Donnie's helmet.

After his kickoff sailed out of the end zone, Kelly found himself playing defense for the first time in his life. The fatigue from the 90-yard run settled his nerves. As he surveyed Anna's offense, Donnie thought, "Dad would get a kick out of this."

On the snap of the ball he read a toss to the Coyote's 200-pound running back, who had scored twice on the same play in the first half. As instructed, he ran full speed downhill and struck the ball with his face mask, causing a fumble which was scooped up by Gunn, who carried it in for a score.

The sudden turn of events sent a rush of adrenaline through the Panther sidelines. The poor first half showing, coupled with the previous year's beating, had cast a pall over the team. Suddenly, hope was in the air.

Coach Dozier's decision to place Gunn at fullback to lead block for Williams, led to two more touchdowns. Late in the fourth quarter, Avina found Nobriga on a slant route tying the game at 28.

With 25 seconds left on the clock, Anna's quarterback saw his wide receiver open on the Van Alstyne 20, when the Panther corner slipped and fell down. He launched the pass fully expecting a game winning touchdown, when out of nowhere came the white shirted number 8 to intercept the pass. Donnie ran the ball back to Anna's 38 with only 4 seconds left on the clock.

"Coach Miller, I can make the field goal," Don told his mentor during the timeout.

"Kelly, that's 55 yards."

"He will make it," promised Coach Guerrero.

Michael studied his assistant's facial expression. "What the heck, field goal team," shouted Miller.

While the Panthers were lining up for the try, the coaches from Anna were screaming, "Watch the fake, watch the fake." The snap from Mike James to his holder Avina was on target. Don struck the ball perfectly. Every eye in the stadium watched the ball tumble end over end, for what seemed to be an eternity. The hush of the crowd was broken when the ball split the uprights.

As the Panthers rushed the field to maul their kicker, Miller turned to Wylie, "Best wrong turn you have ever taken coach." The two elated coaches shook hands.

"He is something else, isn't he? I've never seen anything like this," Jack said smiling.

Chapter 16

The cooler than normal early September morning was refreshing as Don sat on the porch swing reading his Bible. This daily 6 a.m. routine gave his life stability. He had been alone a lot in his life, but lately he was lonely, which was something he had not experienced much. The quiet was broken by a vehicle coming up the driveway. He didn't recognize the late model Ford. When the driver exited, a smile came over Don's face. "You didn't think I was going to miss your birthday, did you?"

Don met his father on the bottom step of the porch. "Hey, Dad," he said with obvious affection. "I sure have missed you."

"Same here, son." As they broke their embrace, the Colonel said, "So I hear you are playing football."

"Yes sir. We have a game tonight."

"If I'm not busy, I might check it out," joked James. "Let's go inside, and I'll cook you breakfast for your birthday."

Having his dad in the "Father's line" nearly brought the younger Kelly to tears. Their eye contact made verbal communication unnecessary. The four year hiatus from athletic competition made this moment special for them both.

Don played an exceptional game. He returned the opening kickoff back for a touchdown, intercepted two passes, caused a fumble, made eighteen tackles and kicked a 47-yard field goal. His only punt on the night went 57 yards in the air. The Panthers finished their preseason record 3-0 with the 35-7 victory over Bonham.

After the game, the Warrior coach Kenny Lamb, approached Donnie. "That was the most impressive game I've ever seen someone play." As the two shook hands, Lamb continued, "Coach Miller tells me you have never played football before. Is that true?"

"Yes, sir."

"How can you play so well, so fast?" asked the wary Coach.

"Coach Wylie says because I have never played; I have no bad habits. He also says I have a nose for the football."

"I'll say," said the admiring mentor. "Good luck, young man. "I'll keep an eye on you."

By the time Donnie's conversation with Coach Lamb ended, the fans were on the field mingling with the players. As Don waded through the congratulatory crowd, he saw who he was looking for standing near the south goal posts away from the masses. "Well done, hot shot. It was a joy watching you compete."

"Thanks, Dad." James wrapped his big arms around his son.

As the two broke their embrace, the Colonel joked, "It looked like you were showing off out there."

Don smiled, "I was trying to impress someone."

"Not me, I hope."

"No, no, no. It was that guy over there," said Donnie, pointing at some random man wearing a warrior t-shirt.

"I have always said you had your mother's sense of humor. Go shower. I'll see you at home."

….

Saturday morning Donnie woke up to the smell of bacon. The Colonel had been up since dawn. In those two hours, he had his quiet time, ran two miles, and made a phone call. He and Donnie had stayed up until almost 1:00 a.m. catching up.

"Good morning, son. Grab a plate and help yourself to Mimi Kelly's famous breakfast."

"Oh, yeah," said Don rubbing his hands together. "She was a great cook, wasn't she?"

"She definitely knew her way around a kitchen, that's for sure"

Father and son ate and talked until Donnie had to leave for his 10 a.m. film session and workout. When he returned, there was a black F150 with a flatbed trailer hooked to it in the driveway. There was a fully covered vehicle on the trailer. As Donnie walked past the trailer, he noticed the truck had Tennessee plates.

74

About the same time, his dad and Riley Sprowl walked out onto the porch. "Hello Mr. Sprowl."

"That's Riley to you."

"Hello, Mr. Riley."

Riley looked at James who shrugged his shoulders and smiled. "Riley brought your birthday present."

Don turned around to look at the covered vehicle. "Is that it?" asked the hopeful 18-year-old.

Riley limped past Don, punching him in the arm. "Yes it is, boy." As the cover was pulled off, Donnie's jaw dropped. A maroon 1969 Ford F100 short bed truck was revealed. The chrome rims with baby moons glistened in the Texas sun.

"Is, is this grandad's truck?" stammered Donnie.

"It sure is, son. Isn't she beautiful?"

"How did you find it?"

"That's where RJ comes in. After Mimi's funeral, Riley hunted down Doug Haro. Believe it or not; he still had it." James continued, "Get this Donnie, he sold it back to me for the same amount he gave mom all those years ago."

"But, it's got to be worth more than that!"

Shaking his head in the affirmative, the elder Kelly agreed, "Thousands more. Mr. Haro is a very generous man, Donnie boy. He also said he would give it to me for nothing but knew I wouldn't take it."

"He insisted on paying for my gas to bring it out here," added Riley.

"Sounds like a great guy," suggested Don.

"Oh yeah, I almost forgot," said Riley while reaching into his back pocket. "Doug told me to give this letter to you Donnie."

The young man opened and read the letter aloud:

Dear Don,

I've never met you, but I knew your grandparents and your father. Your bloodline is strong and faithful. Floyd and Ellie were

75

special people, son. When I bought the truck from your grandmother, I had a feeling I was to keep it for some reason. I was asked to sell it several times over the years, but it never felt right, even though I seldom drove it. So it wasn't a surprise when Coach Sprowl contacted me about the truck and put me in touch with your dad. I am a blessed man, Don, and I truly believe God used me to keep this truck until it could be returned to its rightful owner. Look inside the glove box and you will find a check for the amount your father paid me for the truck. Please use it as you feel led. I hope you sense your grandfather when you drive it.

May God bless you,
Doug Haro

There were several seconds of thoughtful silence before it was broken by Riley Joe. "Let's get this beauty off the trailer."

The interior looked almost showroom new. Donnie stood peering inside with his hand on the door handle. As he turned to look at his father to make a comment, he noticed the Colonel was in deep thought. It was at that moment when he realized how much that truck meant to his father and how selfless he was to track it down for him.

"Dad…. Could you show me how to drive this?"

Instantly the Colonel snapped out of his trance and happily said, "Absolutely. This is a standard three on the tree. Hop in and let's take it for a spin."

As Donnie reached over his right shoulder, James laughed. "There isn't one, son; they only have lap belts." James continued: "You have to choke it to start it when it's cold." He demonstrated the procedure while turning the key, which was on the left side of the steering wheel. The 302-cubic inch engine quickly started and purred like a kitten.

As James revved the engine, Donnie exclaimed; "Ooh, I love that sound."

"Dad put those pipes on years ago," reported James.

76

The Kelly boys drove into town drawing looks from some of the townspeople. They switched places and Don drove back to the house after his on-the-fly lesson. He was a quick study, which brought a satisfied smile to the Colonel.

"I think I'll park this baby in the barn so I can keep it cherry for *my son.*" Donnie parked the F100 and turned to his father. "Thank you, Dad. This is the best birthday gift ever!"

The three men spent most of the day fishing the pond. The non-stop conversation covered the past, present, and future. The evening was spent eating the catch of the day, while watching college football.

Donnie sat in Mimi's favorite chair absorbing all he could. It had been a while since he wasn't either alone or lonely. Today, he was neither.

Chapter 17

The final day of Colonel Kelly's stay had quickly come. He packed his bag and headed back to Sheppard Air Force Base. He made a stop in Whitesboro to watch Donnie play his first district game before continuing on to Wichita Falls. His transport to Ali al Salem Air Base in Kuwait would be leaving early the next morning.

James sat quietly in the stands watching the Panthers win their fourth consecutive game 17-14. Paul Gunn tackled the Bearcat fullback on the one yard line to end the game. Travis Williams led the offense with 128 yards rushing and two touchdowns. Don had another great game with 15 tackles, 2 more interceptions, and a 52-yard punting average. His most impressive contribution was a 56-yard field goal on the final play of the first half.

While Don's teammates visited with their friends and family, he walked his father to his vehicle. The grass stained number 8 stood eye to eye with the Colonel. "It was great having you around for a few days, Dad."

"Just think of what I would have missed," said James nodding toward the field.

"I'll admit I really loved having you in the stands."

"Donnie, I know I've told you that sports are what you do, not who you are. That's still true, but son, you do what you do extremely well," James said with a wink.

"Kelly, the bus is leaving soon," yelled Coach Taylor Penn.

James hugged his still padded son. "I love you Don Floyd Kelly."

"Love you too, Dad."

The two separated, and Don started to jog toward the bus when a sudden heaviness in his heart stopped him. He turned back toward his father who was still standing by his truck. They stood for several seconds looking at each other from a distance of approximately thirty feet without saying a word. James was experiencing similar capricious emotions. With his eyes watered,

Donnie hit his chest with the side of his fist and then pointed at James with the same hand. The normally stoic Colonel mimicked his son's signal of love and affection.

The sight of the white jersey number 8 jogging away brought an audible whisper from the surprisingly troubled father, "Lord, please give my boy strength."

Coach Jaycee Guerrero read Don's countenance when he boarded the raucous bus. He had watched the father/son interaction from the window and sensed that the young man didn't feel much like celebrating.

"Hey, Kelly, sit by me." Jaycee stood and directed Don to sit by the window then sat next to him.

Don acknowledged the coach's discernment with a simple, "Thank you coach."
The emotional battle going on in the young man's heart and mind went unnoticed by his excited teammates during the nearly one hour drive back home.

. . . .

Don walked into the, once again, empty house around midnight. His malaise had been replaced by hunger and exhaustion. He grabbed a box of Honey Nut Cheerios from the cupboard and a gallon of milk from the fridge. When he sat down at the table he noticed an opened envelope. Inside he found the check for $4,500 and a note which read:

> *This is the check from Mr. Haro. Remember, he said to use it as you see fit. I'll be headed for Kuwait in the morning. Remember our usual discussion about who to contact if something happens to me. Also remember, we are both in God's hands, and no one dies early. I love you, Dad*

Don was used to the content of the note. It was, however, the first time it was written down by his father. Everything seemed different this time to Donnie.

79

He audibly chastised himself, "You are just tired, Kelly. Quit being such a wimp." With that, he headed upstairs to bed.

Chapter 18

The next five weeks flew by. The Panthers won all five games, clinching a playoff spot. Coach Brent Loganbill's undefeated Commerce Tigers were on the schedule for what would be the District Championship game.

The final practice on Thursday was the season's best. The excitement of a possible District Championship was obvious. The team was at full strength with the return of center Mike James and outside linebacker Jimmy Gatto, who had missed the last two games due to injury. Robert Randall returned on week five and was moved to strong safety, while Donnie continued to play free safety.

The Panther secondary was labeled the *No Fly Zone* by Jack Walker, the local Sports Reporter. In the last 6 games, the secondary gave up no touchdown passes and had an incredible 17 interceptions; led by Don Kelly's 12, which gave him 15 on the season.

The segment clock's horn blast indicated the end of practice. The team gathered around Coach Michael Miller. "Gentlemen, tomorrow will be the day we have worked for since last season ended." He looked at his players who were positioned in front of him on one knee, with his assistant coaches standing behind them. "We are healthy and we are ready. I am so proud of the hard work and effort you have displayed this year. Get a good night's sleep, and tomorrow we will travel over to Commerce and ruin their Senior Night.

"Oh yeah, let's do this," yelled, the always exuberant Coach Dru Murray.

The team stood and raised their helmets; Armando Avina yelled, "Pride on three. One, two three." The echo of the team's response reverberated throughout the empty stadium.

......

Don turned onto his gravel driveway and parked the '69 in the barn. He closed and locked the door and made his way to the front porch. A vehicle was coming up the drive with two occupants.

When Don noticed the Government plates, his heart sank. The two men exited the blue Lincoln wearing Air Force Dress Blues. "Don Kelly?" asked the passenger.

Don could feel his heart beating out of his chest. "Yes sir," he replied trying to muster a strong voice.

"I'm Colonel Tim Bryant, son, and this is Captain Ron Kumler. Can we go inside?"

The weakness in Donnie's legs made him unsure of his ability to make it inside. "Help me, Lord," prayed Don silently. He unlocked the door and invited the two men inside. "It's my father, isn't it Colonel Bryant?"

The Colonel and Captain Kumler made eye contact, then turned their eyes toward the waiting young man. "Yes, son. Your father was killed last night."

During their twenty minute conversation, the officers were unable to give Don any details because of the ongoing investigation. They did, however, tell him that the base was attacked from the outside, and that there were other casualties.

As the Officers were leaving, Colonel Bryant handed Donnie his card. "Please keep this and call me tomorrow afternoon. I should have information for you concerning your father's body. I would like to help you with the funeral arrangements, if you don't mind."

Don accepted the card, "Thank you, sir. I would appreciate your help."

"Good. I'll talk to you tomorrow." Standing by the car door, the Colonel added, "We knew Colonel Kelly well and can tell you he was a credit to his uniform."

Captain Kumler added, "But, after meeting you, I think his greatest work was as a father."

Donnie stood watching the military vehicle drive away feeling numb. When the tail lights disappeared, he went inside to call Coach Miller.

Donnie was on the porch swing when Michael's headlights

appeared. There was a chill in the November night that went unnoticed by the teen.

Coach Haynes was with Coach Miller as they approached the door. Jimmy Haynes was the logical choice to accompany Miller. He had experienced the loss of two family members and could empathize with Don. His example of strength and courage was well known in the small community.

"I'm over here, Coach." The dim porch light struggled to reveal the young man on the swing.

The coaches approached Donnie, who was still seated on the swing, and sat down on the nearby navy blue rocking chairs with cardinal red *Ole Miss Rebels* emblazoned on the curved back.

"My Mimi bought those when my dad played for the Rebels."

"They are in good shape" noted Michael.

"Mimi didn't have much, but she took great care of what she had."

Coach Haynes decided to deal with the 'elephant' on the porch by asking, "Do you feel like talking?"

There was a brief moment of thoughtful silence before Donnie responded. "Before y'all arrived, I was sitting here looking at the moon's reflection on the pond. I was thinking about all the times Dad and I spent fishing and talking. For some reason, I recalled the story about how he met Mom and how much he was smitten by her." Donnie continued. "It was at that moment that I realized that my parents were together for the first time in 18 years. In my mind's eye, I saw mom running toward him with her arms wide open. My dad loved my mother, Coach. How can I feel bad knowing that they are together again? Don't get me wrong; my heart is broken, but thinking of them being together almost makes me happy. Is that wrong?"

Coach Haynes cleared his throat and answered, "What you are experiencing is a selfless perspective. You see your dad's passing as a reunion, and that can be a very comforting view point. From experience, I can tell you that there will be times when that isn't the perspective you will have. There will be times when you will be overwhelmed with emotion. Don't be surprised if you experience anger. It is all part of the healing process. The most important lesson I learned was, when you feel lost, run *to* God, not *from* God."

"Thank you, Coach. That really helps."

Michael interjected, "Don, no one will expect you to go to the game; so please know that the guys will understand and that they will play their hearts out for you." Don nodded. "Also remember there is no school tomorrow because of teachers in-service. I know you will have a lot to do, so let us know if we can help in any way."

Donnie rose from the swing, indicating that he was ready to end his evening. He hugged both coaches and thanked them for coming, then headed into the house to get some much needed sleep.

Chapter 19

The players were asked to meet in the team room when they arrived. The room was abuzz with anticipation of the championship game. The coaches came into the filled room and stood in front behind Coach Miller. As Michael told the team about Donnie's dad, the excitement was replaced by disbelief and concern for their teammate.

When Miller finished, a cacophony of questions filled the room: "Where is Kelly now?" .... "Is he playing tonight?" .... "When is the funeral?"

Miller raised his hand to quiet the team. "Gentlemen, I'll tell you what I know at this point. I haven't seen Donnie since last night, and I don't know when or where the funeral will be. As far as the game goes, guys, we are going to have to come together like never before. Remember our word of the week: Persistence."

The players looked at each other trying to figure out how to handle this unforeseen circumstance. After a few quiet seconds, Paul Gunn stood up. "Tonight, we play for Donnie. On your feet, gather up." The team huddled with their hands clasped over their heads. Paul led the charge, "For Donnie, one, two, three."

"DONNIE!" yelled his teammates.

While the players were loading their equipment in the trailer and boarding the buses for their trip to Commerce, the coaches remained in the coaching office to discuss their next step.

"Has anyone talked to Kelly today?" asked Dru Murray.

"I've called him twice and left messages, but I haven't heard from him," answered Haynes.

"That poor kid is literally alone," mentioned Jack. "I actually don't know anyone who is the sole remaining member in a family. The sad thing is that, by all indications, it was a great family."

Coach Haynes' cell ringtone interrupted Wylie. "Hello. Hey, Don." All eyes were on Haynes. "No sweat. I understand." There was a pause. "Okay, Monday in Mississippi." There was a longer pause. "Of course." Jimmy looked at the coaches and smiled. "I will wait for you. Okay, see you soon."

Coach Haynes disconnected and addressed the eager staff. "He is on his way back from Wichita Falls. He was making funeral arrangements with a Colonel Bryant. The funeral will be Monday in Mississippi. He said he called a man named Riley Sprowl who was his contact if something happened to his dad. Mr. Sprowl told him that his father would have wanted him to play. Donnie asked if he could still play if he missed the bus. I told him I would wait for him."

"We are whole again," said Murray.

"Let's not tell the guys," suggested Miller. "It will be like a shot of adrenaline when he shows up." All agreed.

The Panthers came off the field after pregame and headed to the visitor's locker room. The team gathered for their normal final pregame talk from their head coach. The coaches congregated outside for their final briefing before Miller joined the players.

Coach Haynes and Kelly came rushing around the corner.

"Are you okay to play, Donnie?" asked Miller.

"Yes, sir."

"Noticing the travel bag hanging from Don's shoulder, Miller ordered; "Suit up." Michael had an epiphany and added, "I want you to give the pregame for me tonight." Don hesitated for a moment and then agreed.

The players were stunned to see Donnie walk through the door. The room went quiet.

"Hey guys." The young men didn't know what to say to someone whose father just passed away. "Last night I thought that I had lost the last member of my family. I couldn't sleep until I realized that YOU are my family now. They say that family support is what a person needs in times like these. What I'm trying to say is: I need you. Let's go win this thing."

As predicted, a shot of adrenaline filled the room. Coach

Miller opened the door and commanded, "Let's go."

The team attacked the door leaving Don to get dressed. The Panther's number 8 dressed as quickly as a stage actor making it to the field in time for the coin toss.

The opening kickoff indicated what Commerce had in store for them. Donnie lofted a high pooch kick to the 20-yard line. The receiver caught the ball, and before he could take a step, was separated from the pigskin by special teams player Lonnie Price, who also recovered the fumble.

On the first play from scrimmage, Avina found Nobriga in the corner of the end zone for a touchdown.

The tsunami-like momentum continued into the second half. By the time the fourth quarter started, the 3rd ranked Tigers found themselves behind 38-0.

Don Kelly played like a man on a mission. He ran the second half kickoff back for a touchdown, giving him 3 on the year. He set a personal best of 24 tackles, with two causing fumbles. Don also intercepted his 16th and 17th passes for the season. Finally, his 58-yard field goal was the longest in the nation. Don's performance earned him the Texas 3A Player of the Week award for the second time on the season.

Chapter 20

The November weather was colder than normal in the Mississippi Delta. The light rain beat on the canopy covering the small gathering for Colonel James Kelly's funeral.

Colonel Bryant had arranged for the body to be delivered to NSA Mid-South in Millington, Tennessee. He and Captain Kumler accompanied the Colonel's remains. Once they arrived at the base, the casket was placed in a hearse and delivered to Memorial Garden Cemetery in Clarksdale, Mississippi. The small crowd included Riley Sprowl, Doug Haro, and the Castle brothers, who made the journey with Don. There were also ten local veterans who came to pay their respects to a fallen comrade.

Pastor Dennis Henderson came out of retirement to perform the third funeral for the Kelly family. The graveside service was closed with a 21 Gun Salute which nearly overwhelmed Don. Two airmen took the American Flag from the casket and folded it. They gave it to Colonel Bryant who, in turn, presented it to Don. "Don, your father was truly the finest leader I have ever known; I am sorry for your loss." Donnie accepted the flag, fighting his emotions.

The local VFW Post hosted lunch for the attendees. Donnie was encouraged by the stories of his father and grandfather that were shared with him during lunch. Doug told stories about Floyd Kelly that Don had not heard before. The new information brought a renewed respect and appreciation for his grandfather. An added perk for Don was his opportunity to thank Mr. Haro in person for his grandfather's truck.

Riley Sprowl called Donnie over and introduced him to a Japanese man wearing a dark suit. "Donnie, this is Paul Hayashino."

As the two shook hands, Donnie recalled; "You went to school with my dad!"

"That's right. I was playing ping pong with James when he saw Becky for the first time. I have never seen someone fall for a girl like your father did for Miss Rebecca."

"Amen," chimed in Riley.

Paul reached into his coat pocket and handed Donnie a picture of his parents. His father was in an Ole Miss football uniform with his arm around his mother. "I took that picture after the Arkansas game where ole Kelly intercepted 3 passes, putting himself in the record books. Those were the happiest people together I have ever known."

"You come from good stock Don. Your dad will be missed," said Sprowl. "By the way, your dad told me to tell you: "Don't be common. He said that you would know what that meant."

Paul handed Donnie his card. "This is my contact information. If you need anything at all, give me a call."

After the Colonel's two closest friends left, Don was approached by Pastor Henderson. "Son, I want you to know that it was a privilege and an honor to be asked to perform the Kelly funerals. I also want you to know that I will not be doing yours. You can do mine," he said with a wink.

The Monday night flight landed at 10:30 pm at DFW Airport. By the time the Castle brothers dropped Donnie off at his house, it was after midnight. Fatigue had taken its toll on Don. He was asleep within seconds after his head hit the pillow. Tomorrow his life as the last of the Kelly family would officially begin.

Chapter 21

Tuesday morning came early for Don. His physical and mental exhaustion weighed heavily on him. Because of the November cold, Donnie had his Bible study at the kitchen table. His focus was hampered by thoughts of his father and the loneliness that kept creeping into his mind. While trying to quiet his mind, Don recalled something his father had told him, "When it rains, everyone gets wet, so all we can do is honor God in our response." Don drew a deep breath, blew it out and said quietly, "Let's go."

School went by without much fanfare. Most of the students didn't know if they should say anything to Donnie, so most didn't. The exception was Caren Korabek. Caren was a conscientious junior who had matured through the responsibility of taking care of her eighth grade brother Charlie. Their single mother had to work nights which required Caren to assume the role of family caretaker. Her father was killed in Iraq when she was 13.

Caren exhibited no self-pity, despite the fact she and Charlie were poor. She learned to sew at a young age and made sure she and her little brother were always clean and well groomed. Unfortunately, her responsibilities after school negated any extracurricular activities. On weekends, she would walk to work at Diamond's grocery store. Charlie was a good athlete and kept out of trouble by being involved with sports. Caren loved him dearly and sacrificed for her brother.

Caren stopped Donnie in the hall after their Physics class, "Don, I'm sorry to hear about your father. I can empathize with you and your loss. My father was killed in Iraq when I was younger."

Don was usually quiet in class and had only spoken to Caren when they worked on a project in class. "I'm sorry, I didn't know that about you," apologized Don.

"That's okay, a lot of people aren't aware. We moved here two years ago, and I haven't shared that information much." She continued, "I understand you have a strong faith. If that is the case, you can make it. I sincerely don't know how anyone makes it alone without faith."

"I appreciate you sharing that we me, Caren. It really does help to be reminded that I am not truly alone."

………..

Football practice went well for the Panthers. Preparation for the playoffs seemed to be more fun than work. No one on the team had experienced playoff football. Coach Miller and his staff arrived the year prior and instilled a positive mindset and a work ethic designed to reach goals. Being undefeated District Champions went far beyond any expectations.

As the team broke the practice ending huddle, Avina tossed Kelly a football, "I'll bet you can't hit the goal post from here, Kelly."

Don looked at the post which was about 40 yards away. In response, Donnie challenged, "See that garbage can over there?" He said pointing at a can at least 60 yards away. "I'll put this ball inside that can."

"From here?" asked Armando.

The entire team had stopped to enjoy the interaction. "That's right," answered Don, "and if I do, you bring donuts for everyone at tomorrow morning's workout."

"And if you miss?" questioned the quarterback.

"If I miss, I'll buy."

"You're on, sucker," said Avina rubbing his hands together.

Donnie started to throw and then stopped and turned to Armando, "Last chance to back out."

"Just throw the ball; it's getting cold," replied Armando.

Don turned back toward the garbage can and tossed the ball in an arcing trajectory. To everyone's amazement the ball went dead center into the can.

"Ohhhhhhhhhhhhhh," roared his teammates and coaches.

Armando dropped his head in disbelief. "You are a freak, Kelly," stated the admiring quarterback.

Coach Penn turned to Coach Murray and said, "I'll second that."

Chapter 22

The Bi-District Championship game vs. Boyd High was played at Flower Mound Stadium. The Panthers were favored to win and did just that.

Avina threw two touchdown passes to Nick Nobriga, and Travis Williams gained 154 yards scoring twice. Paul Gunn caused a fumble that was scooped up by Donnie for a score. Kelly continued his attack on the Van Alstyne record book with 2 more interceptions, one of which he returned for a score. He also knocked down three other passes and caused another fumble.

The only negative to the game was the loss of Williams to a sprained ankle early in the fourth quarter. The 42-0 victory bought the Panther Seniors another week of football.

....

The coaches gathered at the Athletic Training Center on Saturday.

"Do you think he can learn the plays in four days?" asked Coach Miller.

Coach Wylie responded, "I've never seen any high school kid study film and pick things up faster than Kelly. He sees things that other people don't see."

Coach Guerrero added, "When I asked him what he looks for, he says he looks for tells. He picks up tendencies like, how fast the receiver leaves the huddle, or if he secures his gloves. Remember the game against Lone Oak, where he caused three fumbles and made four tackles behind the line of scrimmage, against that stud running back they had?" asked Jacey rhetorically. "He said he saw, on film, that when he was getting the ball his head would be up and when he wasn't, his head would be down."

"I'll add something" chimed in Taylor Penn. "On one of our bus rides, Kelly told me he learned sign language, working with deaf kids, on mission trips he took when he lived in California. He said it helped him figure out what the opponents were trying to communicate to each other."

"I've got him in my Government class, and I'll be honest, he knows more than I do," laughed Jimmy Haynes.

"Well, he did score a 35 on his ACT Test," noted Dru Murray.

"Okay, so y'all are saying he can learn the plays in four days." The coaches laughed at the obvious sarcasm of their leader.

. . . .

The Area Championship opponent was Caddo Mills. The Foxes had a very formidable defense led by middle linebacker, Miles Branson.

The first quarter was a dog fight. Both offenses struggled to move the ball with any consistency. Donnie kept the Panthers in positive field position with two 50-plus-yard punts. The Panthers scored first on a 72-yard punt return by Don, who was filling in for Travis. Scott Heaton started the game in place of Williams at running back. The undersized sophomore ran hard but was stymied by the vaunted defense of Caddo Mills. Heaton fumbled on a vicious blow by the Foxes' D1 candidate Branson. Miles picked up the ball on the Panther's 15 and ran it in for a score.

Caddo took the lead when Avina was sacked in the end zone for a safety—once again, by Branson.

Trailing 9-7 at the half, the coaches decided it was time for number 8 to try his luck at running back. On Don's first carry, he met Mr. Branson in the gap and found himself flat on his back.

"Don't come my way again, or you're gonna get hurt," promised the 245-pound linebacker.

"Run the same play," demanded Don in the huddle.

"Coach Dozier, wants to run a flood route," answered Avina.

"Trust me Armando," I'll take the blame.

"Okay then, zone right," ordered the wary quarterback.

On the snap of the ball, Branson read the zone and headed for the gap; what he did not expect was to find himself on his back with number 8 stepping on his face mask as he headed for the end zone

94

for an 81-yard touchdown. Dropping the unsuspecting linebacker was less of a surprise than how easily Donnie outran the Foxes' secondary.

As Avina made it to the sideline, he apologized to Coach Dozier, "Sorry coach. Kelly asked for the ball, and I couldn't help myself."

"I'll let it go this time," smiled Justin, tapping his quarterback on the helmet.

The momentum shifted to the Panthers who scored on their next three possessions.

Donnie finished with 10 carries for 222 yards and three touchdowns. His 20th interception of the year ended the game with a final score of 35-9.

The coaches were relaxing while the players showered. "Did any of you know Kelly was THAT fast?" asked an impressed Coach Miller.

"He wasn't with us when we timed everyone in the forty," reminded Jaycee. "I'm really curious how fast he is on the watch."

Coach Murray snapped out of what appeared to be a trance, "Is there anything this kid can't do?"

"I've been coaching over 25 years and haven't seen anything like this," said Jack. "He's got the leg of a professional kicker; hits like battering ram; runs like a cheetah; has the instincts of a seasoned veteran; and is smart as a whip. Who intercepts twenty passes in a single season, for crying out loud? If I weren't seeing this myself, I wouldn't believe it."

Chapter 23

Practicing Thanksgiving week is a goal for Texas high school football players. It means you are deep in the playoffs and among the best teams in the state. Another positive, to a high schooler, is the week off from school.

Donnie used the time to deliver wood he had been cutting during the year. Serving his community became a source of great joy for the young man. At first, he performed this particular service to please the Colonel, but after seeing true appreciation, Donnie realized why his father wanted him to sweat and sacrifice his time for others. James would often remind his son that the world did not revolve around him and that the sooner he learned that fact, the more joyful he would become.

On Monday, Colonel Kelly's personal effects, including his truck, were delivered to Don at his home. The 18-year-old now owned 3 trucks outright and knew that 3 vehicles for one teenager was poor math.

On his way home from his last delivery, Donnie stopped at Diamond's to get some groceries. Caren Korabek was his checker. Their conversation was long enough for Don to learn that she was working every day, except Thanksgiving, and that her mother had Thursday and Friday off. As he was leaving the store, Donnie was struck with an idea. As the thought banged around his head, a broad smile crossed his face.

He drove home, put up the groceries, and grabbed an envelope full of the money he had hidden in Mimi's shoe box. He jumped back into his truck and drove to Bill and Vonda Castle's house. Don presented his idea to Vonda and asked if she would be part of the plan. She enthusiastically accepted and took the envelope with $4,500 inside.

"Okay, let me go over this one more time; I go to the Korabeks, give Kathryn the envelope, and tell her nothing. If she asks anything, just tell her it's an early Christmas present from a blessed person."

"Exactly," said Don giving her an okay sign. "Please, Miss Vonda, I don't want Caren to know it came from me. I don't want her to be uncomfortable around me or feel like she owes me anything."

"I'll take it to my grave." said Vonda making a *Scout's Honor* sign with her fingers.

Don had his Mimi's truck full of wood by 9 a.m. He had washed and detailed the Black Ford F150 after having Thanksgiving dinner with the Castle families the day before. After making sure Caren was at work, he filled up the gas tank and headed for the Korabek's. Charlie answered the door. "Hey you're number 8, Don Kelly, aren't you?"

Caught somewhat off guard, Donnie stammered, "Um, uh, yes I am. And you are Charlie Korabek, number 22 aren't you? I've seen you play, and I've got to say, I'm impressed."

The eighth grader was temporarily speechless when the tables were turned on him. A big smile came over his face. "You've watched me play? That's awesome."

"Who is it Charlie?" came an approaching voice.

"It's Don Kelly, Mom. He's number 8 on the varsity football team."

Kathryn Korabek came to the door wearing Levi's, boots, and a sweatshirt with MARINES stenciled on the front. Her brown hair was pulled back in a ponytail revealing a kind face. "Hello, Don, how can I help you?"

"May I talk to you outside, ma'am?"

Kathryn looked toward her son, "Charlie, could you finish cleaning your room please?" sounding like more of a demand than a request. Charlie acquiesced and headed inside.

"Mrs. Korabek, I was wondering if you would like to make a purchase?" pointing to the 3 year old vehicle.

Kathryn looked at the truck full of wood. "How much?"

"$100," answered Don.

"So, you want $100 for a truck load of wood? That's not a bad deal."

"No, ma'am, I'm asking a $100 for the wood and the truck."

Kathryn took a double take. "Did I hear you right?" asked the perplexed single mom.

"Let me explain. My father recently died overseas and left me his truck. I already had this one and another old one, so I don't need another. Mrs. Korabek, we have something in common; we've both lost a loved one serving our country. I am convinced that your family should have this truck. And the wood," added Don with a smile.

Tears were rolling down Kathryn's cheeks, "I don't know what to say, son."

Don took out the signed title from his back pocket and handed it to the teary woman. "You don't have to say anything; just sign this, and it's yours." The pause prompted Donnie to add, "It's all God's anyway."

Mrs. Korabek took the title and hugged Don. "God bless you, Don Kelly."

Don and Charlie emptied the truck and stacked the wood. Charlie jumped in the bed of the truck and started sweeping out the dirt and bark.

Donnie met Kathryn at her porch. She handed him a crisp new $100 bill. "I would appreciate it, Mrs. Korabek if you didn't tell Caren how much you paid for the truck. I don't want her to feel weird around me."

"I get it. I'll just tell her it was a good deal," she said with a big smile.

Paul Gunn pulled into the driveway. "There's my ride."

"Good luck in the game tonight," yelled Charlie from the back of the truck. Donnie waved, got into the Land Rover, and headed to the school to leave for the night's Regional Championship game.

Chapter 24

The Redwater Dragons' bus arrived as the Panther players were taking their travel bags out of the equipment trailer. The first three players off the bus were the Inderbitzen triplets. Rick, Ron and Randy were 6'6" and weighed around 290 pounds each. They were verbally committed to play at LSU the following year. The tattooed trio was well aware that they were intimidating figures and used that fact to their advantage. As the rest of their teammates exited the chartered bus, they stood next to each other arms folded revealing massive biceps. They looked at the Panther players, then at each other, and laughed. Rick asked, "Which one of you is Avina?"

Several Panthers looked at Armando who had his #11 bag on his shoulder.

Rick pointed at his #55 jersey, then at his brothers' #66 and #77. "The triple doubles will be coming for you, so you might want to notify your next of kin." All three laughed at Rick's threat as they walked away.

The Inderbitzens were as advertised. Their bravado was easily backed up with ability. The first half was a hard hitting affair that ended with the score tied 7-7. Avina was harassed incessantly by the triplets and ended up having his index finger, on his throwing hand, dislocated on the Panthers last possession of the half.

"I can't grip the ball coach," informed the Panther QB during halftime.

"Can you play defense Armando?" asked Coach Wylie.

"Yes, sir, and I want to real bad."

Rock King had reset the dislocation and buddy taped it to his middle finger. "He can play defense," confirmed Rock.

"Randall is our backup, so let's just have him switch with Avina." Coach Dozier added, "I think we need to put Gunn in the backfield; we need more protection."

"Sounds like a plan, men. Let's do it," agreed Miller.

The Panthers first possession in the second half started on

their own 20. When Randall came out to quarterback, Rick Inderbitzen loudly commented to his teammates, "Hey look boys, #11 has had enough; now it's number 15's turn." Rick increased his volume, "Hey fellas, do you think his parents have life insurance on him?"

Gunn looked at his quarterback, "Don't listen to them Robert; just give Donnie the ball and I'll lead the way." Coach Dozier was on the same page and called Donnie's number four times in a row. After those four plays, the Panthers found themselves with a first and goal on the Dragon 5-yard line. Gunn scored on the next play, giving Van Alstyne the lead.

The Panther defensive intensity had not waned since the first half. The Dragons were forced to punt on their next three possessions without gaining a first down. Randall hit Nobriga on a 40-yard touchdown pass on a 4th and 1. The surprise pass play seemed to place the Panthers in the driver's seat with only 8 minutes to go in the game. However, the 21-7 lead evaporated in 7 minutes and 30 seconds.

The Dragons scored on a perfectly executed wheel route for a 60-yard touchdown and scored again with 30 seconds left to go in the game, when Donnie, punting from his own end zone, had his first blocked punt of the year, which was recovered by none other than Rick Inderbitzen for a touchdown. The Dragons went for the two point conversion by placing Rick and Ron Inderbitzen in the backfield to lead their quarterback on a lead off tackle. The successful try gave Redwater a 22-21 lead.

The ensuing kickoff was, once again, kicked out of the end zone leaving the Panthers with a long distance to go with very little time. Randall was sacked on the 10-yard line on the first play forcing Van Alstyne to call their last time out with 23 seconds left on the clock.

"Coach, let's do the *garbage can*," offered Avina.

"What's the *garbage can*, Armando?" asked the confused

100

head coach.

"Put Nobriga split out right and Randall split left with Gunn in the backfield to protect Donnie. Have Kelly sprint out right and throw it back left to Robert who delays before sprinting down the sideline."

"That's going to be close to a 65-yard throw," said Coach Dozier matter- of-factly.

"I can make the throw, coach," stated Don flatly.

"Okay then, let's run *Garbage Can,* " ordered the coach while making air quotes.

On the snap of the ball Donnie sprinted to the right with Paul in front of him and Nobriga on a dead sprint down the sideline. As instructed, Randall delayed, causing the corner to divert his attention to the backfield. Robert kicked in the burners and broke into a full sprint down the numbers just as Donnie set up and launched the ball downfield toward the opposite sideline. An eerie silence came over the crowd while the ball was on its distant journey. Randall's catch ignited an ever increasing crescendo as the fans watched him finish his race to the end zone, for what would be the game winning touchdown for the Panthers.

The raucous locker room was quieted by the shrill sound of Coach Miller's Fox 40 whistle. "Gentlemen, that was amazing. I love how you play without fear of failure. Speaking of that, I would like our assistant offensive coordinator to make sure this Regional Championship Trophy makes it back to VA." The players looked at each other perplexed, knowing there wasn't an assistant OC. Coach Miller raised the Gold Football, "To Armando Avina, our Garbage Can OC. Ready, clap" After the team performed their three clap tribute, Avina proudly accepted the trophy.

The hour and a half ride back home from Sulphur Springs would be quite enjoyable for the Regional Champions.

Chapter 25

The next game moving the Panthers toward state championship was in Harker Heights, Texas.

"Welcome, ladies and gentlemen, to Harker Heights Stadium for the Texas 3A semifinal game between the Mathis High Pirates and your Van Alstyne High Panthers. I'm Bill Benton with my partner Byron Whitaker on KXII radio."

The Panther's radio men continued their pre-game commentary, "Well Byron, this has been some ride for the Panthers. The Regional victory over Redwater was simply incredible. I've never seen a high school player throw the ball as far as Don Kelly did on the winning touchdown."

"Coach Miller told me that the winning play was called 'Garbage Can,' and that it was devised by injured quarterback Armando Avina on the sidelines," informed Whitaker.

"I'm convinced one of the reasons for their success this year is that they believe in each other." Benton continued, "We've been doing this for over twenty years, Byron, and I've got to ask you—have you seen anything like the impact one individual can make on a team like that of Don Kelly?"

"Every player is playing better this year, and I truly believe this young man is a major reason why. The most notable is Paul Gunn. He was a very good player last year, but this year he has been exceptional and, according to his coaches, has become an excellent leader."

Bill grabbed the stat sheet from the table, "Let's look at Kelly's contribution on the field this year: he started out as a kicker only, for the first game and a half. Ever since the sudden illness of Robert Randall, he has been on the field defensively, where he has 20 interceptions, 9 caused fumbles, 6 fumble recoveries, 15 passes knocked down, 198 tackles, and has 5 defensive touchdowns."

"That's incredible," said Whitaker shaking his head.

Bill continued, "I'm not finished. When Williams was out for two weeks, Don ran for 403 yards with 4 touchdowns and threw that game winner to Randall."

Byron took over, "Then in last week's quarterfinal game against Mineola, he played part time at quarterback in the Wildcat formation and ran for another 110 yards with a touchdown. To top it off, he was 8-8 passing for 2 touchdowns."

"Fans, we're still not finished with this young man's contributions to this dream season," Benton remarked. "He has been the top punter and kicker in the entire nation."

"Get this, Bill. I looked it up: his punting average would be tops in the country in college as well. All this from a kid who had never played football until this year, ladies and gentlemen. Those that know Don Kelly's story can't help but root for the young man."

Benton concluded, "That's our pregame show; we'll be back for the kickoff after these messages from our sponsor, GCEC Electric."

The Mathis Pirates brought in their state leading rushing game. Their option oriented offense gained an average of 440 yards per game on the ground, led by 230-pound running back Danny Coffman. Coffman passed the 2,500 yard mark in their victory over Cameron Yoe the week before.

The stage would be set for the highly anticipated rematch of last year's State 3A Championship Game against Halletsville, if the Pirates could dispatch the Panthers. Last year's game went into double overtime with Halletsville winning on a two point conversion pass to Kenny Simpson, the McDonald's All American receiver.

The Pirate defense shut out 10 prior opponents in the previous 14 games, including a 35-0 victory against Redwater earlier in the year.

Undefeated Mathis was ranked second, behind Halletsville, since week one and was laser focused on a rematch with the Brahmas.

103

Just before leaving the locker room for the kickoff, Coach Miller took out a newspaper clipping from his back pocket. "This is from the Mathis News." Michael read the highlighted portion of the article, "The Pirates leading rusher Dan Coffman responded, 'No one has stopped our running game yet, and we certainly don't expect Van Alstyne to stop us.'" Miller folded the article and walked out of the room.

"Thanks again to David McGinnis and GCEC for their continued support of Panther football," said an appreciative Bill Benton. *"Byron Whitaker will recap the first half."*

"Thanks Bill. The game got off to an explosive start with Don Kelly returning the opening kickoff for a touchdown, giving the Panthers a 7-0 lead. The Pirates were stopped on their first possession on a 4th and goal on the Panther one by Paul Gunn. Don Kelly kicked a 45-yard field goal on their next possession giving Van Alstyne a 10-0 lead. The key play of the drive was a 22 yard run by Travis Williams.

"The Pirates had a short 25-yard drive for a touchdown after a 51-yard punt return by Douglas McCreath, late in the second quarter, cutting the VA lead to 10-7 at the half.

"The offensive leaders for the Panthers were: Williams with 8 carries for 38 yards; Avina had 4 completions on 9 tries for 52 yards .

"The Pirates were led by Coffman's 44 yards on 10 carries and McCreath's 22 yards on 5 carries."

"Thank you, Byron. The Panther defense has definitely stepped up to the challenge. Were you aware that this is the first time the Pirates have been behind at halftime all year?" asked Benton.

"No," answered Byron, *"I didn't, but I'll bet it has a lot to do with Jack Wylie's defensive scheme. He is playing with three defensive backs and has freed up Kelly to do what he calls "freelance." He told me earlier that Don was a voracious film watcher and is excellent at picking up tendencies."*

"Kelly has 9 tackles so far, so it looks like it's working, Byron. It doesn't hurt to have Avina and Williams back at full strength either," added Bill. *"That's your halftime recap; we will be back after these messages from KXII."*

The fourth quarter started with the Panthers in tight punt formation and Donnie standing on the 1-yard line. VA was trailing 21-10 and the momentum had shifted to the Pirates. To the surprise of everyone in the stadium, Donnie took the snap and headed to his right, eluding the charging punt blocker; finding nothing but turf and the Pirate punt returner, who Kelly easily avoided, on his 99-yard touchdown run.

When the hammerheads were gathered on the sideline, Coach Miller gave a questioning look at Donnie who said, "You said at halftime to never be afraid of losing. I was just following your advice."

"That is what you said," confirmed Coach Guerrero, slapping Michael on the back.

Mathis only gained two yards on their next two possessions but still held on to the 4-point lead with sixty seconds left.

After their final timeout, the Panthers broke the huddle on their sidelines and ran to the line of scrimmage at midfield. Donnie was in the Wildcat formation with Randall split out on the left and Nobriga on the right. Mathis was expecting the *Garbage Can* play and moved their safeties outside the hash marks to assist the corners. Coach Dozier had hoped for this and placed the speedy Scott Heaton at tight end.

On the snap, Donnie dropped back, looked left, then right and then threw it down the middle to a streaking Heaton who caught the ball behind the covering linebacker and took it in for the go ahead score.

Forty-eight seconds later, the Panthers found themselves bound for Arlington.

105

Chapter 26

It was the week of the State Championship game, and the coaches had gathered to watch videos of the opposing team and develop strategy.

"Oh my, how do you stop this kid?" asked Jack rhetorically. The 6'5" Kenny Simpson was said to be the top receiver prospect in the nation. He was sought after by nearly all of the top schools. As the coaches watched Simpson make play after play, Coach Wylie repeated his question, "No, really, how do we stop this kid? Everyone has double teamed him, and he still has well over 100 catches and 30 something touchdowns."

"Part of the problem is that they have a good running game as well" remarked Coach Murray. "I talked to a buddy of mine who played them, and he said it's the best offensive team he's seen."

"Did he offer any suggestions?" asked Coach Haynes.

"He said that if you had someone good enough to play Simpson man to man, then you could focus on the rest of their offense, and then you might be able to slow them down." Murray laughed, then added, "He said that person doesn't exist at the high school level."

Taylor Penn confidently stated, "Kelly can do it." The coaches tried to read each other's thoughts concerning Penn's statement. "I know I'm the youngest coach here, but I've never seen someone do what Donnie has done. I don't see any reason why he can't do this; besides, what have we got to lose?"

Coach Miller went into his office and called Don. When he returned, he was met with expectant looks from his staff. "That young man is not normal. I asked him what he thought of the idea, and he told me that he figured we would go that route, so he has been watching videos on Simpson." Michael held up his hand before anyone could respond. "The interesting thing was that there was no fear or false bravado. I heard almost no emotion in his voice."

"Have any of you seen him exhibit emotion?" asked Jack.

"He's an iceman," suggested Jaycee.

"Do you think he's a ticking time bomb holding all the rage inside?" questioned Dru.

Coach Haynes took the floor, "If you could have seen Kelly the night we found out about his father dying, then you wouldn't think that. He just has an incredibly strong faith." Looking at Michael, "Wouldn't you agree with me, Coach?"

"Yes, yes I do. I've learned a lot about handling adversity from Don Kelly. He inspires me."

"You just inspired me Coach," said Justin Dozier. "Do you remember Kordell Stewart? He played for Colorado, then the Steelers. The one nicknamed 'Slash'?" All the coaches indicated they remembered. "Donnie is our *Slash*. I think he's proven he can learn every position, so let's take full advantage of that fact. He's already played running back and quarterback. I say let's use him as a wide receiver and tight end. You know, move him around. Maybe that would cause some concern for Halletsville."

"I'm all for it, Coach Dozier," indicated the head coach. "We need something. These guys look nearly unbeatable."

"He's the most physically fit athlete I've ever coached, so I don't see a problem there," added Jack.

Chapter 27

The small town was abuzz with anticipation of their Panthers playing in the 3A Texas State Championship game at AT&T Stadium in Arlington. Handmade signs could be found all over town showing support for their boys of fall. The excitement on campus was for two reasons: the game and the fact that Christmas break started after finals on Friday.

Five buses of student supporters were filled quickly with the *Blue Crew.* The Panthers had a large contingent of student followers for away games, which wasn't unusual for small schools in Texas.

On Friday the two team buses were given a police escort out of town. The community lined the sides of the road cheering and waving, with many holding signs of encouragement. The local fire department used their water cannons to spray water over the buses which added a nice touch. Don noticed the last sign, near McDonald's, as they approached the highway 75 on ramp, which read: "Last person out of town needs to turn out the lights".

"People get into this, don't they?" Donnie said to Paul Gunn who was sitting next to him.

"Are you kidding me? This is Texas, dude. In Texas, it's God, family and football; and sometimes, not necessarily in that order. Aren't you into this?"

"Sure, this is the most exciting thing to happen to me."

"Well, you wouldn't know it by looking at you. Are you even nervous at all?" asked the baffled linebacker.

"What's there to be nervous about? It's not like the loser dies. This is fun for me. I love challenges and competition, but I've been forced to learn perspective my whole life; so I'm going to enjoy this night, just like I've enjoyed this whole season. You see, Paul, whether I play well or poorly, whether we win or lose my job is— and this may sound preachy—but my job is to glorify God regardless."

"You're a strange duck, Don Kelly, but, I'm sure glad you're

108

in my flock!"

"Good one, Paul."

………

"Don Kelly is lining up to kick. It's an onside kick! Lonnie Price recovers the ball on Halletsville's 45-yard line!" screamed an obviously excited Bill Benton.

"Coach Miller is going to pull out all the stops tonight, Bill."

"That's right, Byron. Playing a team like the Brahmas, what have you got to lose?"

"Avina is in the gun formation, Williams goes into motion left, Armando drops back and throws, it's caught by the receiver down the middle; he collides with the safety but keeps his balance, touchdown Panthers! What a way to start the game. Did you get the receiver's number Byron?"

Looking through his binoculars from the press box high atop AT&T stadium, "It's number 8, Don Kelly. Bill, that's a new one on me; Kelly hasn't played tight end all year."

"Well, you did say Miller would pull out all the stops," Benton responded.

………

Starting out on their own 20-yard line, the Brahmas lined up in their normal spread formation with Kenny Simpson split out left of the formation. When Simpson realized that he was being covered man to man, he couldn't help himself, "Seriously, you think you can cover Kenny Simpson by yourself? I'm going to embarrass you, son."

Donnie responded to trash talk for the first time. "I don't know if I can cover Kenny Simpson, but I do know I can cover you."

Simpson jumped at Donnie which brought a flag for illegal procedure.

"Whoops," said Kelly to the obviously frustrated receiver.

"You're mine, number 8, you're mine."

Donnie positioned himself in press coverage prompting a 'go

route' for Simpson. The All American left the line of scrimmage; Donnie turned and ran staying on top of Simpson, placing himself in excellent position to intercept the long pass. Once Donnie intercepted the ball, Simpson's attempt to tackle Kelly afterward failed, which resulted in Donnie picking up Randall, Gatto, and Gunn to block for him on his way to a 'pick six'.

The Halletsville players were in shock and were struggling to maintain their composure. They had never trailed in the previous fifteen games. The Brahmas' veteran coach recognized his team's potential meltdown, so he asked for a time out.

Coach Miller gathered his excited players. "Gentlemen, this is the first time they've been tested. You, on the other hand, have been battle worn and flame tempered. Keep your foot on their throat."

The hammerhead team broke out of the team's huddle and charged to their positions. Don's kick was received on the one yard line by Simpson who headed for the wall being set up on his sideline. He made it to the wall, but did not see the kicker until it was too late. Donnie ran right through Simpson, knocking him completely out of bounds, to the delight of the Panther faithful.

………

"Oh my, what a HIT by Kelly!" shouted Bill Benton into the radio microphone. *"He doesn't hit like a kicker, does he Byron?"*

"Kelly is the hardest hitting high school player I've ever seen, Bill. I'll admit, I would be nervous about my son playing on the same field as Don Kelly."

"The interesting thing is that he has never drawn a personal foul."

"That's true, Bill. I still can't get over the fact that he has never played football before. I guess Don Kelly could be described as a natural."

………

Simpson didn't play the next series, trying to shake off the cobwebs. Halletsville lined up to punt for only the tenth time all year. Don caught the punt on his 32 and returned it to the Brahma 20 before being knocked out of bounds.

Donnie lined up in the wildcat and faked a run only to throw to Nobriga for a touchdown making the score 21-0 with 42 seconds left in the first quarter.

Simpson came out on the next series talking. "You got lucky number 8; it's time to show you what an All American can do."

Thank you, whispered Don to himself. He turned to Randall and gave him a hand signal. On the snap of the ball, Kelly left his press position and sprinted toward the backfield where he met the runner who had just received a toss from the quarterback. The unsuspecting back fumbled the ball which was recovered by Jimmy Gatto.

"What made you make that call, Kelly?" asked his defensive coordinator, when he reached the sideline.

"Simpson was trying to bait me, which made me think it was a run play my way. It was a guess, coach."

"Hey, Jack," Wylie heard his name through his headset.

"Yes, Coach Penn."

"I told you he could do it."

"Yes you did; now stop bragging and get back to work," quipped Wylie.

....

"Yes, Panther fans, you heard it right. The Van Alstyne Panthers are your new 3A Texas State Champions with a final score of 31-7 over last year's State Champions, the Halletsville Brahmas. The story of the game was the defensive game plan by the Panther coaching staff. The decision to play Don Kelly man to man against the best receiver in the country, turned out to be a stroke of genius."

"Yes it was, Bill. Kenny Simpson was thrown to fifteen times and had only three catches for 26 yards. Ironically, Don Kelly had as many receptions from the Halletsville quarterback as Simpson. His

111

three interceptions give him a ridiculous 23 for the year."

"Well Byron, by the looks of the Panther faithful assembled on the field, there might not be anybody left in Van Alstyne."

"Yes, sir, and they saw something special tonight."

"To those fans who could not make it, we say goodnight. This is Bill Benton and Byron Whitaker signing off until next year."

Chapter 28

On the bus ride home from Arlington, Coach Miller sat next to his strangely sullen player. "You okay, Donnie?"

Don turned from admiring the Dallas Skyline, to look at his mentor. "I'm a little worried Coach."

"About what?"

"Football and school have occupied nearly all my time. Now, for the next 15 days, I have neither. Being extremely busy has been a blessing, because I haven't had a lot of time to think about my situation."

"I can understand your concern. Is there any way that I can help?" asked Michael.

"I don't think so. I knew it would eventually happen, and I just have to walk through it."

"Do you have plans for the Christmas break?"

"Yes, sir, I'm going to Olathe, Colorado, to help a friend of my dad's. He owns *Dream Catcher Therapy Center*. They use horses for therapy, and I'm filling in for an employee, so she can be with her family for Christmas."

"Don Kelly, I have never met someone like you. One: you are the best football player I've ever coached. Two: you handle adversity better than any adult I know. And three: you are the most humble and selfless teenager I've ever seen. You make people better Donnie. You make me better."

Don looked at his coach and gave an embarrassed smile. Michael stood up, "Oh, by the way, if you want to play college football, with your grades, SAT score, and talent, you can play anywhere you want." Coach Miller returned to his seat and left Don to his thoughts.

....

"Hey Kelly, there's a babe out front asking for you."

Don stopped packing his belongings and looked at the informer and laughed. "Not funny, Paul."

"I'm not kidding. I think she's that girl at Alabama."

Chill bumps covered Donnie's arms as he finished packing. As he exited the ATC, he saw Cassie standing by her car. A broad smile crossed the brunette's face. Donnie returned the smile and couldn't help but think how beautiful Miss Reynolds really was.

The two embraced, "Hey, Cassie, it's good to see you."

"I watched the game on TV and figured you would be here." Cassamae looked toward the ground and then made eye contact with Don. I came here to apologize to you."

"For what?" said Don with an obvious puzzled look on his face.

"A couple of days after I got home for Christmas break, my parents showed me the game they recorded against A&M. It was then that I realized why I didn't hear from you after that game." Cassie locked eyes with Donnie. "Tell me the truth Donnie. Did you see me with Curt while they were interviewing my coach?"

Don briefly hesitated, then shook his head in the affirmative.

"Oh, Donnie, I'm so sorry I didn't tell you before."

"Cassie," said Don while placing his hands on her shoulders, "You don't have any responsibility to share your relationships with me."

"Let's be honest Donnie. A girl knows when a guy is interested in her in that way. And, unless I'm mistaken, you were interested in me."

Don's face turned a light shade of red as he diverted his eyes. "You're right, Cass. You have a place in my heart, but I know you have never led me on or anything like that. After taking a deep breath, he continued, "I'll admit, it hurt a little to see you with him, but I don't want you to feel bad. You haven't done anything wrong."

Don took his hands off her shoulders and gently wiped a single tear running down her face. "Don Kelly, you are such a great guy. I don't ever want to lose you as a friend."

"Not possible Cassie," stated Don confidently while pointing

114

to his heart. "Is he a good guy?"

"He is, Donnie. You would like him a lot."

"That's good. All I know about Curt Burns is he is a great quarterback."

"He was raised right and is well grounded," informed Cassie.

Changing the subject, Cassie said, "I had no idea that you were such a good football player. The TV announcers couldn't get over the fact that you had never played before this year."

Showing a touch of discomfort, Don admitted, "My dad always told me to listen to those who know, and these coaches know what they are doing. All I did was listen."

Cassie looked at her watch, "Donnie, I have to go. Please call me every once in awhile to let me know how you are doing."

After promising to call, Don kissed Cassamae on the forehead, then opened the door to her car. "You are a class act Cassamae Reynolds. I'm glad to be your friend."

Chapter 29

Early the next morning, Don tossed his packed bag into the back of the truck and headed for Olathe. His plan was to drive to Pueblo, Colorado, spend the night, and then finish the drive to the little town on the western slope of the Rockies. The December weather was unseasonably mild which encouraged the 18-year-old, who had some concern driving the 900 miles during the winter.

Two and half hours later, Don made it to his favorite taco stand in Wichita Falls for a breakfast burrito. He found himself standing behind an airman carrying a duffle bag. Donnie got the attention of the server and signaled that he would pay for the airman's order.

When informed of the gesture, the surprised serviceman turned to Don and nodded in appreciation.

After receiving his burrito and large coffee, Don looked for a place to sit. "You can join me," offered the airman who was already half way through his meal.

Don offered his hand, "I'm Don."

"Carlos Herrera," responded the airman, shaking Don's hand.

During the conversation, Don learned that Carlos had just returned from overseas and was headed to Pueblo via a Greyhound bus, from the station across the street.

"I'm going through Pueblo and can drop you off, if you want to save some time and money," suggested Don.

"That sounds better than riding a bus. I'll take you up on the offer."

Three and a half hours later, Don pulled into a Texaco station outside of Amarillo.

"Do you want to drive?" Don asked. I need a break."

"You're going to let a stranger drive your truck?"

Don laughed at Carlos' comment and responded, "After four hours of stories, I don't consider you to be a stranger anymore."

After refueling, the Ford F150 headed north on highway 87

116

with a new driver. After several minutes of silence, Carlos asked, "I'm a little confused. It's Christmas break and you are heading to work for someone 900 miles from home. Don't most people spend the holidays with family?"

Don looked out his window at the barren Texas panhandle without responding. Thinking his question was out of line, Herrera apologized, "Hey, man, I'm sorry if I said something wrong."

Donnie turned to his new friend, "I don't have a family Carlos."

All Herrera could muster from Donnie's revelation was a barely audible, "Oh."

A light rain started falling forcing Carlos to turn on the wipers. All that could be heard was the steady movement of the blades until Carlos couldn't keep quiet any longer; "I'm sorry for my curiosity, Don. Have you been an orphan all of your life?"

Donnie simply replied, "No".

"Do you mind sharing your story?" Carlos asked cautiously.

Don gave the 'Readers Digest' version of his life.

When he told the part about his father, Herrera's jaw dropped. "You're Don Kelly, aren't you?" blurted Carlos.

Goose bumps instantly covered Donnie's arms. He knew he had not given his last name to Herrera. The look on Don's face was enough to confirm the assertion.

"I knew Colonel James Kelly. He was my Commanding Officer." The 18-year-old stared at his driver in disbelief. "Don, your father saved my life," said the young airman with a crack in his voice. Carlos took his eyes off the road for a moment to look at his passenger.

"Our barracks were bombed in the middle of the night. I was knocked unconscious in the blast. I came to when I was lifted onto someone's shoulders and carried out of the burning building. That someone was your dad, Don. He had already saved two others before me.

"The Colonel was tending to me when a scream for help came from the building. Your father left me with a medic and sprinted into the building toward the scream." Don could feel his quickened pulse rate as he listened to Carlos. "Before your father could get out, the building collapsed."

"When we were finally able to remove the debris...." Herrera could barely speak, wiping tears away from his face. Once he regained his composure he continued. "When we removed the debris, we found the airman on top of your father only ten feet from the door." Realizing this was the first time Don had heard anything about his father's death, Carlos asked, "What did they tell you about your dad?"

Trying to recollect the conversation with the two officers, Don offered," It was the day after, and all they knew was that he and some others were killed. They didn't have the details at that time."

"Well, I was there and if it wasn't for your father, there would have been three more dead airmen."

Don turned toward his window absorbing Herrera's tale. Again, the only noise in the cab came from the wiper blades as the pair entered the city limits of Dalhart, Texas.

235 miles later, Carlos parked the truck in front of the Herrera's home. "It's getting late. Please consider spending the night with us. My parents have a guest room, and my mother is a great cook," bragged Carlos. Being emotionally drained and physically tired, Don agreed to stay.

Carlos Sr. was an adept storyteller with a dry sense of humor. It had been a long time since Don had laughed with such abandon. He actually felt better than he had in quite a while. After a breakfast of chorizo and eggs, Donnie headed toward his final destination.

Young Kelly had a great appreciation of history and wanted to take advantage of the journey down historic highway 50. He stopped in Canyon City to check out the Holy Cross Abbey and the Colorado Territory Prison Museum. Before leaving the area, Don visited the Royal Gorge Suspension Bridge. The view of the Arkansas River from over 1,000 feet made him feel small.

As he continued his journey, Donnie found himself over 11,000 feet elevation as he traveled through the Monarch Pass on the Continental Divide. About an hour later, Don reached Gunnison, which he determined was his favorite place on his trip. Finally, after a day of majestic views, the small town of Olathe came into view.

Chapter 30

Don turned right onto the gravel driveway after seeing the metal sign bearing the name *Dream Catcher Therapy Center*. At the end of the driveway was a shotgun style house with a wraparound porch. The house was painted white with black shutters. Behind the house was a 200x80 foot covered riding arena next to the barn which housed the horses. Kathy Hamm ran the Center. Bill taught government at the local high school and also was a sergeant in the Colorado National Guard.

Don met Sergeant Hamm when he had a three-hour layover at DFW. James took Donnie with him to meet the man who had set up the blind date with his mother.

Bill was standing on the porch with a cup of coffee. "Mr. Kelly, you look just like your daddy did back at Ole Miss. It's a little eerie to tell the truth."

"Actually, you are one of only two people I know who knew my father back then. So, I can honestly say you are the first person to say that to me."

"He was the real deal, Don," added Mr. Hamm. "Grab your bag and come on in and meet my girls."

The first to meet Donnie was Alli. Her features and size clearly revealed Down's syndrome. "Hi, I'm Donnie. What's your name, beautiful?"

She shyly responded, "Alli."

"Pleased to meet you, Miss Alli."

She could not help notice Don's scar. "What happened to your face?" she asked.

Kathy Hamm made her way from the kitchen wiping her hands on a towel. "Alli!"

Don laughed, "It's okay; I get that a lot." Returning his gaze to his inquisitive new friend, "I was in a bad car accident a few years ago."

"Does it hurt?" she asked sincerely.

"No, sometimes I forget it's even there."

"Hello, Don. I'm Kathy. Lunch is ready, so I hope you are hungry," she said returning to the kitchen.

After lunch, Bill took Don on a tour of the property. Inside the barn was a tack room adjacent to a small bedroom. "This will be where you'll bunk. It will give you some privacy."

Don noticed the pictures on the wall. Pointing to one of a younger Bill in an Ole Miss baseball uniform, "Did you play ball at Ole Miss?" asked a somewhat surprised Don. "You didn't tell me that at the airport."

"It just never came up, I guess. I was a relief pitcher."

"I'm planning on playing baseball this year," informed Donnie. "My injuries have kept me from playing until this year. I love baseball."

"I've got an idea," said Bill as he walked over to a footlocker at the end of the bed. He lifted the lid and retrieved two baseball gloves and a ball. "Want to play some catch?"

"Absolutely," was Donnie's reply as he caught the glove Bill had tossed to him. The two went into the arena. Bill flipped on the lights revealing a much larger area than Donnie had expected. He looked up at the fans on the ceiling. "Wow, those are huge fans."

"Actually, they are Big Ass Fans," said Bill laughing. "The brand name is "Big Ass Fans".

"Now that's funny," admitted Don. The two played catch for about fifteen minutes, finishing with a little game of burnout.

"I enjoyed that," said Bill as they headed back to the tack room. "It's been a long time since I've played catch."

"You still have a good arm, that's for sure. Look how red my hand is," said Don while showing him exhibit A.

"Compared to you, young Kelly, my arm is weak. Do you pitch?"

"I used to. I haven't played since I was fourteen."

"Tomorrow, I'll show you how to throw a sinker. It was my

best pitch."

"Can't wait, Mr. Hamm."

Bill and Don rose early the next morning and headed for the barn. They fed and watered the horses and cleaned the stalls. After breakfast they headed to Grand Junction with a pickup load of hay. Hamm supplied hay for a few customers during the winter months.

The three hour round trip provided Don the opportunity to learn more about his parents when they were young. Hearing about them from another's perspective was very educational for the young man. Bill spent a lot of time with James and Becky during his tenure at Ole Miss, and his ability to spin a tale gave Donnie a ringside seat to his parent's past.

The work was hard and consistent. Running a business involving horses required diligence and time. Bill took advantage of Donnie's presence to make repairs to the barn and stable on top of the daily routine.

Despite their fatigue, the two men played catch every day. Donnie was beginning to master the sinker Bill had taught him days before.

"Don, I've got to say, you are a workhorse. It's good to see a teenager who isn't afraid to sweat. You've been a great help these last five days."

"Mr. Hamm, I needed this more than you could know. You have shared things with me that I never knew about my parents."

"Speaking of parents, could you do this one a favor?" asked Bill. "Alli asked me if you would take her to Montrose to shop for Christmas. She wanted to buy her mother something without her knowing."

"I would be honored, sir. She's a sweetheart."

Chapter 31

The next day Donnie took Alli to the River Landing Shopping Center in Montrose. "Mom is going to love this," Alli said, without trying to contain her excitement, while showing Donnie the necklace she bought with her own money. "I can't wait for Christmas to get here." Alli grabbed and held Donnie's hand as they left the jewelry store and headed for Sports Authority for her daddy's gift.

She bought her father a St. Louis Cardinals baseball cap, "My daddy loves the Cardinals, Mr. Don. He's going to be so excited to get this," giggled Alli as they left the store and headed down the sidewalk. Out of the blue she said, "I love it when Daddy calls me 'AlliBama'."

About the time Don was going to reply to Alli's revelation, she was knocked down by one of three older teenagers coming out of a boxing gym.

"Watch where you are going, you little freak!" shouted the perpetrator who was covered in the soft drink he was carrying.

Ignoring the outburst, Donnie brought Alli to her feet. "Are you okay?" asked Don quietly.

Alli gave a wary look at the angry teen, noticing a dragon tattoo on his arm. She hugged Donnie while whispering, "He's scary."

"Dude, your girlfriend needs to watch where she's going; look at what she did," pointing at his wet shirt. The two other teens stood with their arms folded trying to look tough.

"It was an accident; besides, you ran into her," said Don calmly.

"Bull shit, this little gnome ran into me." The other two laughed at their friend's insult.

Don replied without emotion, "This girl is a child of God, and I would appreciate it if you wouldn't curse around her."

"A child of God!" laughed the teen, "Well, God screwed up on this one."

123

"That's a good one, Buck," said one of the other teens.

"Well, *Buck,*" said Don with a touch of sarcasm, "You must be a lost soul, so I know you can't help yourself."

Filling with rage, Buck threatened, "I ought to kick your ass right here."

Don seemed to be enjoying himself as he retorted, "Proverbs does say that a quick tempered man does foolish things; and trying to kick my ass would be very foolish on your part."

"Let's take him inside and teach him a lesson," suggested the previously quiet teen who was pointing at the boxing gym door.

"Look guys, all you have to do is apologize to the lady, and we can avoid this nonsense," boldly stated Donnie.

"That's not going to happen, pal; what's going to happen will be painful for you, smart ass," predicted Buck.

Don turned toward his shaken companion, "Alli, sit on that bench over there, and I'll be back in a few minutes. Everything is going to be just fine."

Don followed the other three teens into the gym. Buck talked to a man behind a desk pointing at Donnie. The man laughed and shook his head pointing to the empty ring. Still in his workout clothes, Buck pulled out a pair of MMA gloves and climbed into the ring.

"Hey, Bible boy, it's time to meet your Maker," he said, while gesturing Don to join him in the ring.

Donnie removed his jacket and boots and took the gloves handed to him while climbing into the ring. "This really isn't necessary, Buck; all you have to do is apologize."

"Let's do this!" shouted Buck as he moved toward his opponent. Don ducked an anticipated roundhouse kick and sent a devastatingly accurate shot to the jaw which sent Buck to the floor unconscious.

Don stood over his fallen foe shaking his head while removing his gloves. As he climbed out of the ring he made eye contact with Buck's friends. "Gentlemen, my friend is waiting for her apology."

The two surveyed their unconscious companion for a moment and then headed for the bench occupied by Alli.

Alli was so excited to place her gifts under the tree that she did not mention the incident at the shopping center. Donnie was relieved that she didn't remember the situation as it was, and chose to remain silent himself.

Chapter 32

Alli still had her child-like exuberance as she raced downstairs to the tree on Christmas morning. Bill and Kathy were waiting for her with their coffee mugs in hand and smiles on their faces. Donnie sat on a stool observing this small family's tradition.

"I want you to open mine first," implored Alli, as she retrieved the gifts she bought from under the tree. "You first, Mom." She handed Kathy her gift and then clapped her hands.

Kathy opened the box and found a beautiful necklace with a cross attached. With a genuine smile crossing her face, Kathy said, "Oh, honey, this is so beautiful! Thank you so much." She wrapped her arms around her daughter and gave her a warm embrace.

Alli handed Bill his gift and squealed, "Now you, Daddy. Open it, open it." Bill pulled the Cardinals hat from the wrapping and placed it on his head.

"Fits perfectly, AlliBama. It's the best gift ever." The smile on Alli's face was precious to Don as he watched this loving family.

After Alli opened her gifts, Donnie handed her one more. "I brought this for you from Texas. The gift was an Asher Surplus + Flag bag from Stash.

"Wow, this is awesome. Thank you Donnie."

"That bag isn't cheap, Donnie," noticed Kathy.

"She's worth it Miss Kathy."

"I've got something for you, Don," said Bill as he handed him a wrapped gift. Donnie opened the gift to find a picture of a young woman wearing an Ole Miss football jersey. "That's your mother, Donnie, wearing your father's football jersey." Don stared at the picture intently for several seconds without saying a word. Bill continued, "I found that picture in the attic and had it made into an 8X10 when I found out you were coming."

"This is the only picture I've seen of my mother in college."

"We didn't have the technology back then that allowed everything to end up in pictures," teased Bill. As Donnie studied the

126

picture, Bill finished. "She was a special person, Don. Everyone loved her."

....

Don threw his bag in the back seat and headed up the gravel driveway on his way back to Texas. The twelve days he spent with the Hamm family was just what Don had needed. He made his way home carrying knowledge of his parents that he had never known before. It was truly a gap-filling two weeks for young Kelly.

Chapter 33

"Hey, Kelly, come to my office after the workout," said coach Miller, as Don entered the ATC. Christmas break had flown by, and Donnie was looking forward to the last Friday of January, which was the first day for baseball tryouts.

"Yes sir," replied Don as he entered the weight room.

Coach Miller had a stack of slips in his hand. "These are phone calls I've received just today asking about you." He read some of them aloud: "Baylor, Texas, SMU, LSU, Texas A&M, Texas Tech, Kansas State, Oklahoma, Alabama." Miller handed the slips to Don. "There are ten others from all over the South. You are a hot commodity right now, Kelly." Noticing Donnie's lack of emotion, Michael hesitated a moment, then asked, "Do you even want to play college football?"

"Coach, lately I have been struggling with what I want to do with my life."

"What makes your heart beat, Donnie? What gets you excited?"

"That's the problem, Coach; not a lot gets me excited, and sometimes I don't even know if my heart is beating."

The frankness of Donnie's answer confounded his mentor. "I really didn't expect that response, Donnie. I wish I had some magic words for you. All I've got is, pray and ask for guidance."

The winter wind beat against the live oak next to the window, causing the branches to brush against the house, awakening Donnie. When he turned on the lamp, Don saw the phone slips on the stand. He sat up and placed his pillow behind his back and started looking through the slips one at a time. Donnie had prayed all the way home from the ATC asking for guidance. He listened as instructed, but didn't 'hear' anything. He had gone through them several times, but this time one caught his attention. Donnie stared at the school's name on the front and smiled. He placed the slips on the stand, returned his pillow to its proper place, and turned off the lamp. Don Kelly was asleep in seconds.

Coach Miller was in the ATC weight room at 5:30 AM like every weekday. The young mentor had continued his workout routine since his days as a player for Central Oklahoma University. He had just finished his warm up stretches when Donnie walked through the door. Miller waited for his young charge to open the conversation. "Got a second, Coach?"

"Sure do, what's up?"

"I made my decision."

"But you haven't talked to anyone or visited any campuses."

"Yes, sir, but I did what you said, and the answer came to me late last night."

"Tell me it's OU; you know that's where I want you to go," kidded the coach.

Donnie laughed then said, "No sir, I want to go to the Air Force Academy."

"How did you come to that decision?" asked the surprised coach.

"There was one from Mississippi State, which made me think of Ole Miss, which made me think of my dad, which made me think of the Air Force. All that led me to choosing the Academy."

"Well, I can't argue with that Donnie," laughed Michael.

"Do you think I can get in?"

"With your test scores and grades, I doubt you'll have any trouble getting in. Besides, after you left yesterday, the Air Force Academy recruiter called and showed great interest in you. He told me that a guy who knew your dad called him about you. I don't believe in coincidences, Donnie."

"I don't either coach."

………

National Signing day was an exciting day for Van Alstyne. The local TV station and newspapers were in attendance. Signing day was one day where small Texas schools could find notoriety. Six players signed scholarships: Paul Gunn with Texas Tech, Nick Nobriga and Robert Randall with Central Oklahoma, Jim Gatto with North Texas, and Armando Avina with the University of Reno in Nevada.

Because of the rules for the military Academies, Don's signing didn't bind him and allowed other schools to continue to recruit him. As much as he enjoyed the experience, Don Kelly was ready to reconnect with his first love: baseball.

Chapter 34

Coach Jimmy Haynes decided to take advantage of the unusually warm day and have a live scrimmage. Last year's top pitcher, Roger Riley, was on the mound for the blue team and Don Kelly pitched for the white. Riley had already signed with Henderson State in Arkansas and was considered one of the top pitchers in Texas 3A baseball. The Panthers were returning their two top hitters, seniors Kevin Nowotny and Mark Kackley. The previous year, the Panthers were knocked out of the playoffs in the second round and returned most of their hitting and defense. The only missing ingredient for a possible deep run was pitching depth.

"Blue team, hit the field," yelled coach Haynes.

Riley retired the first three hitters which included Kackley. "What were his gun times, Coach Penn?" asked Haynes.

"85 fastball, 76 breaking ball, 68 change. Not bad for this early in the year," suggested Taylor.

Donnie headed for the mound and faced Nowotny first. On the first pitch the lefty drove the ball over the right field fence for a home run. Don tipped his hat to Kevin as he rounded the bases.

"That won't happen again, Nowotny," laughed Donnie.

"We'll see, Kelly," said Kevin as he jogged around the bases. Nine pitches and three outs later, Donnie headed for the dugout.

Coach Haynes looked at Penn expectantly. "91 fastball, 79 breaking ball, and an 86 mph sinker."

Kackley, Donnie's catcher, chimed in, "That sinker is straight up nasty, Coach."

Now standing close enough to Taylor to whisper, Jimmy said, "I've got goose bumps."

The Panthers scrimmaged four other schools during the next two weeks. Donnie earned the starting centerfield position when he wasn't pitching. He exhibited an exceptional ability to get a jump on the ball, and his arm was well above average. The biggest surprise was his hitting. The ball exploded off his bat which made pitchers nervous. He hit two home runs, two doubles and a triple during the scrimmages. The most impressive was the triple, because the ball stuck in the chain link fence just below the 340 sign.

Coach Haynes was most pleased with the pitching. In addition to Riley and Kelly, Nick Nobriga, Scott Heaton, and Frank Gonzales proved to be effective on the mound. Heaton played third base and Nobriga shortstop when they were not pitching. Junior Mike Gase earned the spot at second with his brother, Dennis, filling in at third or short when Scott or Nick pitched. Armando Avina and Nowotny bracketed Donnie in the outfield. Robert Randall filled the remaining position at first, while sophomore Eric Simoni played in the outfield when Kelly pitched.

After winning the first two tournaments, the 8-0 Panthers headed for Tyler to face their biggest challenge of the early season. Anticipating having a quality team, Coach Haynes entered the 4A and 5A tournament in east Texas to test his young charges. The quiet excitement was tangible as they pulled into the stadium parking lot. Neither Roger nor Donnie had given up a run in their two outings and were looking forward to competing against the bigger schools. Roger was scheduled to face 5A Lindale in game two. Donnie was penciled in to face host 5A Tyler Lions in the final game of the tourney.

The Lions were led by senior Blake Hunter. The 6'5" left hander was projected to be selected in the first round of the MLB draft in June. Hunter was 3-0, with a 0.00 earned run average, after throwing four innings in a makeup game on Tuesday. Not wanting to place his star player in jeopardy, Coach Bart Williams decided to throw Blake on Saturday against the Panthers. Hunter's prowess was well known throughout Texas causing mixed emotions to permeate the Panther team when they learned who would be on the mound Saturday.

Thursday's opponent in the round robin tournament was against 4A Chapel Hill. Van Alstyne jumped out to a lead on Don's

132

three run homer in the top of the first inning, driving in Kackley and Nowotny. Scott Heaton pitched well over six innings, leaving the game with the score tied 4-4. Donnie threw out the potential winning run at home plate in the bottom of the seventh, forcing the game into extra innings. Armando Avina scored the lead run on a two out single by Robert Randall in the top of the ninth. Frank Gonzales, who had taken over for Heaton in the seventh, loaded the bases with no outs in the bottom of the ninth.

Standing on the mound with his infield surrounding him, Coach Haynes summoned Kelly from centerfield. Donnie and Eric Simoni tapped gloves as Simoni jogged out to take over the centerfield spot. "We've got ourselves a situation here, young man. What's on your mind?" asked Haynes.

Donnie looked at his infielders, then back at his coach, and smiled. "I'm thinking it will take nine pitches to win this thing coach."

"Sounds good to me," said Gase.

"Me too," echoed Nobriga.

"Well then," said Jimmy, "I'll see you in nine pitches."

Coach Haynes was laughing when he reached the dugout. "What's so funny?" asked Coach Penn.

"Kelly just told me he will finish this thing in nine pitches. And here is the kicker: I think he believes it." After six pitches, the bases were still loaded, but there were two outs. Three pitches later, Donnie had recorded his third consecutive strikeout to end the game. The two coaches looked at each other and shook their heads in amusement.

Chapter 35

Several VA players crossed the street from their hotel to Cici's Pizza. As they entered the restaurant, they drew the attention of the five players from Tyler. Among the group was Blake Hunter, who was wearing an LSU cap. He had signed with the Tigers back in November.

After stacking several pieces of pizza on their plates, the Panther players sat across the room from the Tyler contingent. Several minutes later, one of the players approached and stood at the end of the table nearest to Scott Heaton and Eric Simoni. "What's up, guys? I'm Charlie Wise. I'm the catcher for the Tyler Lions."

Scott did the honors; "I'm Scott; this is Eric, Robert, Roger, and the guy at the end of the table is Don."

"Pleased to meet you, guys." Charlie turned and pointed in the direction of his teammates while turning a chair around and straddling it with his arms folded over the back. "Me and the boys were talking, and we don't think it's fair what is going to happen to you Saturday."

"What do you mean?" asked Scott.

"Well, you guys are probably okay for a small school, but we really don't know why you are even in this tournament. That team you beat today is weak. The two teams tomorrow will beat you easily, and you don't stand a chance against us on Saturday." Charlie turned toward his mates to see them all watching and laughing as he was.

"You sound pretty sure of yourself, Charlie," snapped Roger.

"Well, I know you've heard of that guy over there in the LSU hat. That's Blake Hunter and unfortunately for you, he will be on the mound Saturday. He has already signed with the Tigers and will be a first round draft choice this June. I catch the guy, and he's unhittable." Charlie finished, "Look, you seem like good guys, but that man is dangerous, and to be honest, you are out of your league."

Charlie's sarcastic diatribe angered Scott to the point he was about to rise from his chair and confront the Lion catcher. His plan was thwarted when Donnie reached across the table and firmly grabbed Heaton's arm and shook his head at his friend.

Don set his eyes on Charlie, who was now standing, and spoke in a firm and confident voice. "You say Mr. Hunter is dangerous, but I'll bet he didn't play football because his father and his expensive pitching coach told him he shouldn't, for fear of his getting hurt. In fact, Mr. Wise, I figure his dad has controlled pretty much every aspect of his life to protect his investment. The pressure to perform must make it so difficult to actually enjoy the gift he has been given." The stunned catcher was speechless as Donnie punctuated his monologue. "Finally, *Charlie*, I think you and the rest of the 'posse' just hang around lefty for some future advantage for yourselves. So I really don't think any of you are all that dangerous." Wise seemed frozen as Don and the guys got up to leave. "Oh, and tell Blake that the scouts are going to pay close attention to how he handles adversity. We will do our best to provide some, even if we are just an okay small school," offered Donnie with a hint of sarcasm.

While crossing the street and nearing their hotel, Eric blurted, "That was awesome. I've never heard you talk like that Kelly. I've got goose bumps."

"I hate it when people play head games. That was all Charlie was trying to do. He hasn't even seen us play," explained Don.

"Well, I think you will be in Charlie's head for quite some time, Don Kelly," said Roger. "And if he is dumb enough to tell the others what you said, they will all have *Kelly* on the brain."

135

Chapter 36

Not a word was uttered as the Panthers exited the bus for their contest against the Tyler Lions. The Panthers split their two games the day before and were feeling good about themselves. The Cici's incident was now known by the entire team and the excitement was growing. Several Tyler players had made their attendance known during VA's two games the day before. Their presence and comments were designed for distraction, but ended up being motivation for the small school.

Don Kelly and Mark Kackley were stretching in the right field corner in preparation for their long toss ritual before Donnie pitched. "Look at all those scouts behind home plate, Donnie. There must be nearly twenty."

"I guess it's your day to show off, Kack," teased Donnie.

"Actually, I am a little nervous," admitted Mark.

"My dad used to tell me to concentrate on what I was doing, not how I was doing. With practice, his advice helped me to block out my surroundings," said Don.

"I might need to try that today," laughed Kackley.

As Hunter made his way to the mound, the scouts stopped their talking and pulled out their radar guns. After throwing down to second, Charlie Wise approached the mound. Both players looked into the VA dugout. "Let's show them why they don't belong here," said Wise, before heading back to his position.

Blake struck out Mike Gase on a 95 mph fastball to start the game. Kackley hit a one hopper back to the mound for the second out. Left-handed Kevin Nowotny struck out on a nasty breaking ball to end the inning. "I told you guys that you don't belong here," said Charlie, loud enough for Kevin to hear, as Wise jogged back to his dugout. The Lion dugout was loud and mocking as they met Hunter with fist bumps and high fives.

By their actions, it was obvious that the scouts were more than impressed with what they had just witnessed.

Donnie's first warmup pitch hit the backstop when he slipped and fell during the delivery, drawing laughter from just about everyone in the park. Even Don found the humor in his clumsiness. He picked up his hat that had fallen from his head, and tipped it to the laughing Lion dugout. His next pitches were thrown more for mound familiarity, than for accuracy or velocity.

After Kackley's throw down, he and the infield met on the mound around Donnie. Their pitcher held out the ball and reminded his mates, "This is what we are playing guys, *the ball*, not the Lions. Place our focus on this and we will be fine."

Once his teammates returned to their positions, Donnie threw his first pitch. The pop of catcher's mitt from the 94 mph fastball got the attention of the distracted scouts. The radar guns came out like an old western gunfight. The stunned leadoff hitter didn't take the bat off his shoulder on the next two fastballs of equal velocity and accuracy and was dispatched to his bench. The Lion dugout went silent as they watched their normally aggressive leadoff man frozen in the batter's box.

The next batter swung on the first pitch, not expecting the change up he received, and hit a soft pop up to Nobriga at short. Charlie Wise stepped to the plate and gave Donnie a challenging glare. A sharp breaking ball knocked Charlie on his backside, despite the pitch being called a strike. A faint smile crossed Don's face as he retrieved the ball back from Mark. An embarrassed Wise got back in the box, this time without the glare. Kelly noticed Charlie's forearms rippling, caused by the tightening of his grip on the bat, so he threw a changeup. Wise swung so hard, he nearly found himself on the ground again. A 96 mph fastball on the outside corner ended Charlie's nightmare.

The scouts were buzzing with what they had just seen. "Who is this kid?" was the question of the moment. After much discussion, they determined that no one had ever heard of Don Kelly.

Don stepped to the plate to lead off the second. Charlie

dropped his middle finger and Blake nodded. The 90-plus mph pitch hit Donnie square in the back. His reaction led one to believe that it did not hurt him at all. When he reached the bag, the first baseman quietly said, "That's what you get for having a big mouth."

"Hey, eight," shouted a man, wearing an LSU hat standing next to the first base dugout. "I'll bet that hurt. You must not be very smart talking about my boy that way!"

Don pretended to not hear the comment. On the first pitch, he stole second, beating Charlie's throw easily. After the next pitch, he was standing on third dusting himself off. Wise slammed his mask against his guards before placing it back on his head.

Robert Randall stepped out of the box with a one-one count and looked at the signals from third base coach Scott Ritchie. He positioned himself in the back of the box and squared, giving the impression of a squeeze. Hunter fell for the bait and threw the ball up and in. Donnie was racing home on the pitch with the intention of using the ruse to steal home. His slide was in front of the plate, with his right hand brushing across home; giving Charlie no chance of reaching Kelly in time. The Panther faithful leapt to their feet in boisterous appreciation for the gutsy call; while the Lion followers sat in stunned silence.

When Don stepped to the plate with two outs in the fourth, he was the only player who had been on base. He stayed back on an anticipated breaking pitch and deposited the ball over the left field wall, hitting a parked car over 400 feet away. As he approached first base, Don caught the eye of the man in the LSU hat who dropped his head and headed back to the Lion's side of the stands.

Everyone in the park was witnessing one of the best pitching duels ever seen at the high school level. Both defenses played flawlessly, and the game was only one hour long going into the top of the 7th inning.

When Don stepped to the plate for the third time, he still was the only Panther player to reach base. After striking out twice previously, Nowotny hit a line drive to first for the initial out of the inning. Hunter's first pitch to Kelly was very up and in, causing Donnie to drop onto his backside. The Panther coaches, players, and fans shouted angry protests toward the home dugout. As Don came to his feet, he held out a hand toward his bench, calming his teammates.

"Hey, Charlie," said Don before stepping back into the box, "You might want to go tell your pitcher that if he throws me a strike; he had better duck."

"Knock it off guys," ordered the umpire.

"I'm just trying to be a good sport sir; I don't want him to get hurt," replied Don.

"TIME," yelled Wise as he headed for the mound.

As Charlie and Blake discussed Don's warning, the umpire said, "Son, this kid can bring it, and you've already been hit once. I can't believe you are taunting him like that."

"I'm just trying to get him ready for pro ball, sir," bringing an audible chuckle from the tickled umpire.

Charlie returned to his position without saying a word. On the very next pitch, Hunter threw a 94 mph fastball that Donnie sent up the middle, nearly decapitating the Lion hurler.

After seeing his star pitcher nearly killed, Coach Williams asked for time and headed to the mound to check on his star. He was joined by his infielders, catcher, and the home plate umpire. "Are you okay?" he inquired of Hunter.

"Yes sir," said the pitcher, who was picking up his hat that was knocked from his head.

"He warned him, coach," said the umpire.

"What do you mean, he warned him?" inquired Coach Williams.

"He told your catcher that if he threw a strike, that he needed to duck."

"No way," said the disbelieving mentor.

139

"It's true," admitted Charlie.

Bart just shook his head and asked, "Are you good to go?"

"Yes sir," replied his pitcher.

Before making his next pitch, Blake turned toward Don, who was occupying first, and tipped his cap, drawing a tap of the bill from Kelly. The inning ended on a long fly ball to center by Scott Heaton, leaving Donnie at third after stealing two more bases. Don took the mound in the bottom of the inning and finished his perfect game by inducing two ground balls and a strikeout. The one hour fifteen minute game was one for the books.

Blake and Charlie approached Don after the game, "I apologize for hitting you," said Blake.

"And I want to apologize for being such a jerk to you guys," confessed Wise.

"I guess I can admit this now; it hurt like hell!" said Donnie with a fake grimace. After a few more minutes of small talk, the rivals shook hands and parted.

Chapter 37

Don arrived home after attending church on Sunday to find a box wedged between the screen door and the door to the house. A note was attached to the top of the box which read:

Don,

I am sorry I missed you. This box contains some more of your father's belongings. I am sorry it took so long to get them to you. Sometimes, things in the military are not as proficient as they should be. Hope all is well with you.

Colonel Tim Bryant

The contents in the small box included pictures of Donnie at various ages, and a picture of James, Don, and Ellie on the porch swing. He also found the framed Homer Hickam quote that his father had on his office wall. At the very bottom of the box was a sealed letter bearing Don's name on the front. He opened the letter with some trepidation. The letter was dated after his father's last visit.

My Dear Son,

If you are reading this, then I have gone to be with the Lord. I am so very sorry to leave you at such a young age.

Tears immediately started falling down Donnie's face, disturbing his vision. He took a deep breath, wiped his eyes and continued.

I truly understand the Father's love based on my love for you. I pray daily that He will uphold and keep you. Tap into His strength, because you have none of your own. Son, you are a true blessing to me. The selfless and sacrificial way you took care of your Mimi makes my heart full. Our days of working and fishing are indelibly etched in my mind. Observing the joy you exhibited while playing sports was contagious. By the way, you are one heck of a football player! You are actually better than I ever was.

Don smiled at his father's compliment, certain he was just being a dad.

The adversity you have gone through in your young life is far more than normal. You are not common, Don. God is using and will use your life for others. Remember, Son: anything and everything can be taken from you, except your integrity...you have to give that away. I love you with all of my heart and soul.

Dad

PS: Remember: *"When it rains, everyone gets wet"*

Don allowed the stream of tears to fall. He crossed his arms on the table and laid his head on them. After several minutes, he raised his head and grabbed a tissue from the box in the middle of the table to blow his nose. He took the picture of the three Kellys and placed it on the mantel next to the picture of his mother given to him by Mr. Hamm. He adjusted the picture of his Grandfather Floyd to make all three symmetrical.

Chapter 38

Jackson Arroyo, the Regional Scout for the Texas Rangers, walked into the office of Assistant Director of Scouting, Dave Swift. Dave had just returned to his office with his brothers, Doug and Darren, from having lunch. "Well, I'm here to tell you that the Hunter kid is legit" said Jackson. "I'm also here to ask if you have ever heard of the Kelly kid from Van Alstyne."

Dave thought for a brief moment and simply said, "Never."

"Are you talking about Don Kelly?" asked Doug.

"Yes I am," said the surprised scout. "Have you seen him play?"

"I've seen him play football," answered Doug. He turned to his younger brother, "Darren, that's the kid who played against your boy in the playoffs."

"Oh, yeah, number 8. That kid was amazing. He could do it all," recalled Darren.

"Well, the kid might be a better baseball player," stated Arroyo matter-of-factly.

"How so?" asked Dave.

"I only saw him pitch and hit but, people from Van Alstyne say he is an outstanding outfielder with a cannon for an arm. If that is true, then this kid could be a 5 tool player."

"You said you saw him pitch?" asked Dave.

"Yes, I did. I saw the best high school pitching duel I've ever seen. All Kelly did was throw a perfect game against Hunter's team. He throws low to mid 90s with a nasty sinker and a much better than average breaking ball and change. Offensively, he has great bat control and hits for power. And he might be the best base stealer in the state.

"Where did he come from? What year in school is he?" asked the assistant director.

"According to the roster, he is a senior. I was told that he was in a bad car accident his freshman year and is playing for the first

143

time."

"So you are saying there is a phenom out there that no one has heard of?" inquired Swift.

"Well, he isn't a secret anymore. There were a bunch of us in Tyler to see Blake Hunter. I've been doing this for a long time, Dave, and this kid is definitely worth seeing again."

"What kind of size are we talking about?"

Arroyo thought for a second and said, "I'd say about 6'3 200."

"Well Jackson, I guess you will be visiting the big city of Van Alstyne," laughed Dave.

………..

After the first round of District, the Panthers were sitting atop the standings with an undefeated record of 7-0. The team was clicking at all facets of the game. Riley and Kelly maintained their dominance on the mound. Because the offense was hitting on all cylinders, Coach Haynes was able to use his relievers to keep the starter's pitch counts down. When asked by the media why his team was playing consistently well, Jimmy simply stated, "The boys have determined to play the *ball* instead of the opponent." When asked to clarify, Haynes said, "Consistent preparation develops consistent play, and these kids have bought into that philosophy."

Arroyo parked his red Ford Fusion in the parking lot of Forrest Moore Park to watch the Wednesday practice. He wanted to observe how Kelly practiced and interacted with his teammates without knowing he was being observed. After watching for over an hour, Jack picked up his phone and punched in Dave Swift's number. "Hey, Dave, I'm sitting here in Van Alstyne watching the Kelly kid practice."

"What have you learned?" asked the interested Assistant Director of Scouting.

"I'm not only impressed with him, I'm impressed with the whole team. These guys got it going on. They hustle everywhere and the focus seems game-like."

144

"Do they know you are there?" inquired Dave.

"I don't know how. No one has even looked my way since I've been here."

"Tell me about Kelly," implored Arroyo's boss.

"I would say he could very easily be a five tool player. I have seen him play in the outfield and can tell you that he can go get it, and he has a plus arm. I really think you need to see this kid yourself. Maybe you and I can check him out when the playoffs start in a month or so."

Dave replied, "Sounds good. In the meantime, try to find out this kid's story. I still can't believe no one has heard of him before this year."

"Okay, Dave. I'll go to their game on Friday, incognito, and see what I can find out. Talk to you later."

Arroyo arrived early enough to watch pregame infield. He was dressed in nondescript clothing trying not to draw attention to himself. Sitting behind home plate were three of his peers, notebooks in hand. The success of the team drew larger than normal crowds, which allowed Jackson to blend in. He noticed an elderly man with pad and pencil and figured him to be a sports writer. The man was standing along the third base side fence by himself.

Arroyo stood next to the man about five feet away. "I hear that Van Alstyne has a pretty good team." said the scout, trying to initiate a conversation.

"Yes, sir, they do."

"Are you a sports writer?" asked Arroyo pointing at his pad.

"I am," the reported answered.

Arroyo stuck out his hand, "Jackson."

"Hello, Jackson, I'm Jack," said Jack Walker.

"Great name," said Arroyo releasing Walker's hand. "I heard about this Kelly kid and had to see for myself."

"Well, I have been writing for over 40 years and can tell you he is the best player I've ever seen."

145

"That's saying something," admitted the scout. Arroyo had decided that he had chosen the correct person to learn about Don Kelly. "He seems to have come out of nowhere. Did he move here from out of state this year?"

"Actually, he has quite the story," said Walker.

"Do you know it well enough to share? I love a good story."

Chapter 39

Jackson arrived at Dave Swift's office at 9 AM with two cups of coffee. "Cream, no sugar, right?"

"That's right," said Dave, taking the paper cup offered by Arroyo.

"Well, what did you find out?"

"I talked to the local newspaper guy who had the scoop. I'll give you the short version."

Dave took a long sip from his coffee and crossed his feet on his desk. "Let's hear it."

"Okay, here goes: his mother died giving birth to him. He was severely injured in a car accident when he was fourteen. He lived with his grandmother while his dad was overseas in the Air Force. Kelly home schooled while recuperating. While his grandmother was dying of cancer, he was legally emancipated by his father. Apparently, he was very close to his grandmother. She died around a year or so ago, leaving him living by himself."

"My goodness! This kid doesn't seem to have much luck," uttered Swift aloud.

"I'm not finished. It doesn't get any better."

"You are kidding," said Dave taking another swig of his coffee.

"On the first day of baseball tryouts, last year, he broke his arm saving a woman from drowning."

"Okay, Jackson, you don't have to make up stories to make him look better," joked Swift.

"I'm not Dave. This is legit. The kid climbed into the river, pulled the woman out of a partially submerged car, and broke his arm when they fell backwards onto part of a collapsed bridge." The assistant scouting director started to speak, but stopped when Arroyo raised his hand. "He rehabilitated by using a killer obstacle course at his house."

"You went to his house?"

"No. The writer had interviewed Kelly at his house and took pictures of the course. It is a top notch set up, and here is the best part: he videoed the kid doing a workout. Take a look." Arroyo started the video he received from Jack Walker.

After watching the workout, Dave said, "We are drafting seventh. What are the odds of another team drafting him before us?"

"A month ago, I would have said, *none.* Now I'm not so sure. Don Kelly is becoming quite the *soup de jour.*"

"Wait a minute, Jackson. Why did this guy give you the video? You said you were incognito."

"Well, I was until I swore him to secrecy. I told him who I was, and he promised not to share the information. He really likes this Kelly kid and wants what is best for him."

"Is his father still overseas?" asked Swift, thinking of the next move.

"You are not going to believe this, but his father was killed a few months ago, leaving the boy without any family whatsoever."

Dave just stared at his scout in disbelief before asking. "Did the writer say anything about this kid's emotional stability?"

"He said that the most remarkable thing about Kelly *was* his emotional stability."

"Okay Jackson, you have convinced me. I'll go with you to see him when the playoffs start."

Arroyo got up to leave, but stopped short of the door. "Oh, I almost forgot: Walker also said that Kelly is super smart and that he signed to play football at the Air Force Academy."

"Well, if he is super smart, he won't pass up a six million dollar signing bonus. That's for sure."

"Good point. Talk to you later."

Chapter 40

Don Kelly parked his '69 Ford truck in front of Caren Korabek's house. He put on his tuxedo jacket and grabbed the corsage he had placed on the seat next to him. Donnie took a deep breath and blew it out forcefully. He thought to himself, "Here we go."

Caren's brother Charlie was waiting on the porch for his local hero. "Hi, Donnie. That's a cool truck you have. Caren will be out in a minute. My mom is at work. She had to work a double shift tonight," said the young teen in rapid succession. While Don was digesting the information, Caren stepped onto the porch wearing a navy blue mid length, sleeveless, round collar dress. Her thin snake chain necklace held a simple cross. Not having pierced ears, Caren's only other jewelry was a purity ring her father had given her on her 12th birthday.

"You look very pretty, Caren," said Don handing her the wrist corsage.

"Mom told me to take pictures, so you two get over by the truck," ordered Charlie. After Charlie fulfilled his duties, Don opened the door and helped his date into the truck.

Caren rolled down the window, "Charlie, Mom will be home in an hour. Stay here and call me if you need me. Love ya, bro."

"Love ya, sis."

"My other truck is a lot more comfortable. Someone dressed as nice as you should at least have air conditioning."

"What can I say? I love classic cars. It's something I got from my dad."

Taking advantage of the opening, Don asked, "Tell me about your dad, Caren."

For the next several minutes, Caren reconstructed her life with her father. Don could tell that her father meant the world to her. He also noticed that she twisted her purity ring when she talked about trying to live a life he would approve of.

149

"Your father sounds like he was a great guy. And from what I've seen, he would be very proud of the person you have become." Caren blushed at the compliment, but didn't verbally respond, despite being touched by Donnie's comment.

After dinner at the Three Forks Restaurant in Plano, the couple headed for the Stonebridge Country Club in McKinney. A BMW convertible, with three male occupants, pulled up next to Donnie on the passenger side. "Hey, babe," said the driver to Caren through her open window. "Why don't you dump the jerk and come hang out with us? We'll show you a good time."

Caren burst into fake laughter, "Oh my, you are SO funny. You should have your own TV show."

Don drove away and left the embarrassed driver at the light. "Well, I learned not to mess with Miss Caren, that's for sure."

"You have to hit Neanderthals where they are weak."

"And may I ask, where are they weak?"

"Their EGO, Mr. Kelly."

Five minutes later, Don parked the maroon beauty in the back of the country club parking lot and walked around to the passenger side. He opened Caren's door and held out his hand to help her down. "Why, thank you Donnie. You are such a gentleman." Don bent his elbow so Caren could place her arm in his.

As they approached the door to the country club, a voice sounded from behind: "Hey dude, you need to put a leash on your dog."

Don turned around to see the BMW convertible about 20 yards away parked in the street. "Go inside Caren; I'll be right there."

"That doesn't bother me Donnie. Let's go inside."

"I'm sorry, Caren, but it bothers me. Please go inside."

Don walked toward the driver's side of the car with the same three occupants. The driver tried to get out, but Don stopped him by placing both hands on the door, using his 6'3" muscled frame to keep it closed.

150

"Do you know me?" asked Kelly in a low, confident voice, accompanied by an executioner's stare. He could tell that the driver was staring at his facial scar, which delayed his response, so Don continued. "The answer to my question is 'no'. So, if you don't know me, you also don't know what would happen if I let you out of this car." At that comment, the two passengers looked at each other trying to decide if they should engage. Donnie stared at them and slowly shook his head, answering their silent question.

Seconds later, the door to the country club flew open revealing Paul Gunn, Armando Avina, and Mark Kackley heading toward the car.

Don backed up from the BMW and suggested, "Guys, you might want to leave now."

The BMW exited in a hurry leaving the well-dressed friends standing in the street. "Caren said there was a problem out here," informed Gunn.

"Nope. They were looking for the closest pet store; something about a dog leash," deadpanned Kelly, leaving his friends perplexed as he headed for party. "Let's go have some fun."
....

"I had a great time Donnie. I would never have known you were such a great dancer!"

"My grandmother taught me how to dance when I was younger. I guess it's like riding a bike." Don held Caren's elbow as she stepped onto her porch. The moment of awkward silence was broken by Donnie. "May I kiss you Caren?" Caren nodded her head and Donnie leaned in and kissed her lightly on the mouth. "I had a great time too, Caren. Goodnight."

151

Chapter 41

As promised, Dave Swift accompanied Jackson Arroyo to watch Don Kelly play. Van Alstyne's first round opponent was Grand Saline. The Fighting Indians finished fourth in their district and were underdogs versus the Panthers who completed their district schedule unbeaten. In the top of the first, Kelly crushed a three run homer over the centerfield fence giving the Panthers an early 3-0 lead. In the bottom of the inning, Donnie struck out the side on nine pitches. The dye had been cast, and the Panthers won 10-0 in five innings.

"Well, I've got to admit, the kid is impressive," said Swift as he and Arroyo walked to the car. "I would have liked to see how he handles adversity."

"I've seen him play several times now and can tell you that he has only shown one trait—total focus."

"How can a kid who hasn't played baseball since he was fourteen, go out and perform at such a high level? I don't get it," said the very perplexed scouting director.

"You know Dave, all my life I've heard that baseball is mostly mental. Maybe he just has great mental acumen. It might be just that simple."

"Well, *mental acumen* isn't all he has. He has been gifted physically as well."

"Remember his story, Dave. All he has experienced in his young life, is adversity. Think about it. I'll bet athletic pressure to him isn't pressure at all. Maybe, to him, it is *just a game*."

"Well, that would explain a lot. I've just never seen it in someone his age, that's all."

As the two Texas Ranger employees left the parking lot, Jackson asked, "Kelly will be in centerfield tomorrow. Are you coming with me?"

"Wouldn't miss it, Jackson."

"Well, I guess the secret is out," said Jackson, pointing to a group of men behind home plate. "I see scouts from at least sixteen teams here. There's Tyler Dyer in the front row. He's the lead scout for the Astros. He's known to have a good nose for talent."

"That's impressive, but look who is sitting two rows behind him."

"I don't recognize him, who is he?" asked Arroyo.

"Steve Campbell, the General Manager of the Colorado Rockies."

"I can't remember seeing a GM at a high school game," admitted Jackson. "They draft two spots ahead of us. Is Don Kelly a number one pick Dave?"

"Well, if not, he is moving up quickly."

Kelly ended the bottom of the first inning by throwing out a runner at home from deep centerfield, drawing disbelieving looks and head shakes from the gaggle of scouts. Then he led off the top of the second with an infield single. "Did you get his time to first?" asked Swift.

Jackson looked at his watch, then turned it toward his boss. "3.75; oh my! I've got goose bumps," said Dave rubbing his forearms.

The game ended with Kelly robbing a game tying home run from Grand Saline's cleanup hitter after the Panthers had taken the lead on Kevin Nowotny's home run in the top of the 7th. Don had two triples to go with his single, scoring two runs.

"He looks to be the five tool player you said he was, Jackson. His speed and arm strength are certain. I would also say he plays the outfield like a professional right now."

"His bat speed is also impressive. He kept his hands back and lined that second triple to right field with authority," responded Jackson

"Did you hear the sound it made on that metal wall?" asked

Dave.

"Sound? Did you see the dent it made?" blurted the impressed scout.

"We may not get this kid, but I've had a great time watching him. Thanks for encouraging me to go with you Jackson."

Chapter 42

At the 3A Regional Finals, the senior laden Edgewood Bulldogs featured left-handed pitcher Terry Land. Land, a Baylor signee, took the mound for the Bulldogs in the one game Regional Final against the Panthers' Kelly. The two hurlers battled for six innings without giving up a run. The tension in the large crowd was electric. Donnie stepped up to the plate in the top of the seventh with two outs and Nowotny on first. Land had held him hitless on the day with two strikeouts and appeared to have Kelly's number.

After meeting on the mound with his pitcher, the Bulldog mentor made the decision to pitch to Don. The decision looked to be the correct one after Donnie swung and missed the first two pitches. However, twelve pitches later, Donnie was still standing at the plate with a 3-2 count. Both dugouts were standing, as was the entire, emotionally drained, crowd. After the ninth foul ball, Kelly and Land stood looking at each other. Both competitors appeared to be enjoying the battle. Terry returned the slight nod he received from his current adversary.

With Nowotny on the move for the sixth straight time, Donnie laced a shot into the right centerfield gap on, what appeared to be, a perfectly located fastball. Kevin scored easily with Donnie beating the tag with a head first into third. The Panther faithful were exuberant until Kelly removed his blood soaked batting glove, revealing a lacerated middle finger on his right hand. The third baseman had accidentally spiked Kelly after jumping for the high throw from his relay man.

Coach Ritchie summoned Rock King from the dugout. "He's going to need stitches, Scott. I'm afraid you are done for the day, Mr. Kelly." Eric Simoni replaced his injured teammate at third, while Rock worked on Don in the dugout. Roger Riley took Kelly's place on the mound and closed out the game, qualifying the Panthers for the 3A State Finals in Round Rock for the first time in the school's history.

Chapter 43

Donnie stood in line with his groceries in the cart. "Hey, Caren, how are you?"

"Well, Mr. Kelly, if this isn't a pleasant surprise. I didn't expect to see you until tonight."

"I had to get some groceries for next week." Don gave Caren the cash and placed his bags in the basket. As he started to push the cart toward the door, he turned to Caren; "And maybe I wanted to see you before tonight," said Donnie with a wink.

……..

"Hey, Donnie," asked Charlie from the back seat. "Everyone is saying you are going to be drafted in the first round tomorrow." Don looked in the rearview mirror at Caren's brother.

"Is that true, Donnie?" asked Caren, who was sitting in the passenger seat.

"Coach Haynes has been keeping all the baseball people from me. He does say that there are several teams interested."

"That's so cool," stated Charlie emphatically. "You are like some kind of hero, Donnie. Can I have your autograph?"

Don laughed and said to Charlie, "Baseball is what I do; it's not who I am. So, Charlie, I'm not really any kind of hero. I'm just Donnie."

Kelly pulled his truck into a slot at Founders Plaza DFW. "I thought it would be fun to watch the planes come in for a while, before we eat. You can hear the tower talking to the pilots from the speaker over there." Donnie gave Charlie a pair of binoculars as they exited the truck. "They come in from over there," said Don, pointing to the west. "Look, there's one coming in now." Charlie focused on the jumbo jet through the binoculars while Don and Caren sat on the bench.

"Caren, can I share something with you that has been bothering me?"

156

Caren looked at her brother, who had worked his way further west. "Sure, Donnie, what is it?"

"People treat me like I'm this special person, someone who has it all together. But the truth is, sometimes I feel like a total fraud." Caren's look begged him to continue. "As you well know, being a military brat means moving a lot." Caren shook her head in agreement. "I never felt like I belonged anywhere. It was like I didn't have a home. I would see kids with their moms, and it would make me jealous. Can you believe that? Being jealous because other kids had a mom? That's warped, if you ask me. There was this subtle rage boiling inside me. I acted out in school and would spend many days in the principal's office."

"You don't seem like an angry person now. How did you get over the rage?" Caren asked.

"My dad took me to a VA Hospital, and we spent the day with the vets. I heard their stories and came away feeling embarrassed about my selfishness. My dad never said a word. He just let the experience change my heart."

"I'm a little confused Donnie; that was a long time ago. Why do you feel like a fraud now?"

"Because I don't have it all together," said Don with a little more emphasis than was necessary. "I don't have all the answers. I struggle nearly every day trying to do the right thing or respond the right way. It's exhausting." Don stood up and Caren gently grabbed his arm.

"That's why the Bible says we all fall short. I can see your prideful nature, Don Kelly. I have it too—always trying to be in control of your responses and emotions, trying to measure up." Caren grabbed both of Donnie's hands and looked deep into his eyes. "We both know that that is a fruitless endeavor. Let's agree to give the steering wheel to the One who knows how to drive."

"I'm hungry. Let's go eat," shouted Charlie as he made his way back.

157

Don squeezed Caren's hands, "Thanks, Caren. I needed that reminder."

After eating a sandwich at Weinberger's Deli in Grapevine, the three friends walked around the lighted square enjoying the pleasant evening. "How are you so calm, Donnie? I figured a baseball player in your situation would be super excited."

"It is exciting, Caren, but, to be honest, I'm a little melancholic not being able to share this with my dad and grandmother."

"What's *melancholic?*" asked Charlie.

"It means, *sad,* brother."

"Oh," said the embarrassed eighth grader, lowering his head while shoving his hands in his pockets.

The trio walked in silence for a couple of blocks before Donnie opened the door to Braums. "Anyone for ice cream?" asked Don. Charlie's sullen mood was immediately broken as he headed inside.

Chapter 44

Don finished reading his Bible on the porch swing as the sun rose over the trees. He stood and stretched as he looked toward the pond. His thoughts took him to the glorious days he and his father spent fishing on Mimi's pond. It was there that James Kelly shared life with his son. Donnie smiled as he recalled how his father described the first time he saw his mother. The memories prompted Don to promise himself that he would fish the pond today after practice.

The Panthers were scheduled to practice at 11:00 AM since school ended the week before. Wednesday's trip to the State Tournament had the town buzzing once again. The State 3A Football Championship was still fresh in the minds of the Panther faithful. The possibility of two State Championships in the same school year was euphoric.

Practice was dominated by talk of Kelly being drafted. The draft was scheduled to be televised that evening at 6:00. Coach Haynes had anticipated a distracted team, so he decided to have only batting practice. After Donnie finished his round at the plate, Jimmy called him over to the empty visitor's dugout. "Tonight is the night, Donnie, how are you doing?"

"I'm okay Coach. It really doesn't feel real to me, to tell you the truth."

Haynes pointed to the players on the field. "I think they are more excited than you are."

Don looked at his teammates and then turned to his mentor; "Coach, I…I need my dad." With his voice cracking, Don continued, "This should be the most exciting day of my life, but it doesn't feel that way at all. I actually feel guilty and a little ashamed for feeling this way."

Jimmy reflected on his recent experience and said, "Don't let your guilt and shame paralyze you, Donnie. We all care about you very much. You have truly been a blessing to all of us."

Haynes placed his hand on Donnie's shoulder and changed the subject; "How's your finger?"

Donnie took the bandage off his stitched finger and showed it to Jimmy. "I don't know if I will be able to pitch."

"That's the beauty of baseball, Don. It offers players the opportunity to step up when they are needed. Riley is a gamer; he will do fine."

Chapter 45

Don parked the Gator in the same spot he did when he fished with his father. He set up his chair and threw his line in the water. This would be the first time Donnie fished the pond since the Colonel died. He was hoping to find clarity at the location of his fondest memories. He was struggling and could not figure out why.

After a couple of thoughtful hours of fishing, Donnie decided to work the course since he was still dressed in his hitting shorts and running shoes. He placed his fishing gear in the utility vehicle, took off his Ole Miss tee shirt, and jogged to the nearby course. Don was dripping wet when he finished his routine on the punching bags. He was exhausted, but felt much better. After driving the gator back to the barn, he showered and headed for Paul Gunn's house for a draft viewing party.

"With the fifth pick of the first round, the Colorado Rockies select Don Kelly from Van Alstyne High School in Van Alstyne, Texas." Gunn's house erupted with cheers and high fives.

Kelly was mobbed by his jubilant friends. After everyone calmed down, Nick Nobriga asked, "Did the Rockies call you?"

"I don't know. I left my phone at home."

"You've got to be kidding me."

Donnie shrugged his shoulders and laughed. "You know I hardly ever have my phone, Nick."

"Kelly, are you even a real teenager? I sometimes wonder if you are even from this planet!" scolded Nobriga.

"Hey, Kelly. Do you have to wait until our season is over to sign?" asked Armando Avina.

"I don't know," answered Don. Coach Haynes has been handling everything for me. He didn't want me to be distracted."

"Are you going to get an agent?" inquired Paul.

"I haven't thought about that."

"Well, you might want to start. I understand a first round pick can get a 5 or 6 million dollar bonus." Several of the friends gasped at the number. "That's right, boys. We are friends with a soon-to-be millionaire."

Don checked his phone when he walked in the door to his house. There were several congratulatory messages from well-wishers. The first message, however, was from Steve Campbell, the General Manager of the Rockies:

"Don Kelly, this is Steve Campbell of the Colorado Rockies. I just wanted you to know that we are on the clock and are going to choose you with our first round pick. I will contact Coach Haynes and set up a time to meet. Good luck in your game this week. Welcome to the Colorado Rockies family."

Don walked over to the fireplace mantel and looked at the pictures situated on top. *Dad would be so proud,* thought Donnie. At that moment, Don's ring tone *'Take Me Out to the Ball Game'* sounded. He looked at his phone and saw *Cassamae Reynolds* on the screen. "Hi, Cassie, how are you?"

"I'm fine Donnie. I am so proud and excited for you."

"Thank you, Cass. It means a lot coming from you." The two old friends talked for almost an hour. Don found out that Cassie was still dating Curt Burns, the Alabama quarterback who was recently drafted by the New Orleans Saints.

He also learned that she was going to be at the game in Round Rock. "I hope that is okay with you, Donnie."

"Of course, it is. It would be great to see you," he replied.

Curt is coming with me. He has heard a lot about you and wants to meet you."

"I look forward to it, Cass."

She had heard, through the grapevine, about Caren. "I hear that you are dating someone; is that true?"

Caught a little surprised by the question, Don hesitated. "Well, I, uh, I have gone out with Caren Korabek."

"I know her. She's a sweet person. Are you exclusive?" Cassie laughed, knowing she was making Donnie uncomfortable.

"Come on Cass, you're making me blush. I'm going to be in Colorado, so I didn't think it would be good to start something up. You of all people should understand that."

"Touché, Donnie. Touché."

Besides, Don thought to himself, *you, Cassamae Reynolds, own my heart.*

Chapter 46

At the State Semi-Finals, the Bishop Badgers scored two in the top of the first on three successive doubles. The Panthers went down in order in their half of the inning. Riley settled down and did not allow a run over the last six innings. The Panthers struggled to put anything together. Donnie was intentionally walked his first three trips to the plate, scoring the Panthers' only run on a sacrifice fly by Scott Heaton.

The bottom of the seventh inning provided drama for the large crowd. Kevin Nowotny came to the plate with two outs and runners on second and third, trailing 2-1. With Kelly on deck, the Badgers decided to pitch to Nowotny. The first pitch was driven over the fence, just foul, causing groans from the Panther fans. Nine pitches later, Kevin was standing on first with a walk.

Donnie stepped to the plate to chants of *Rockies, Rockies,* from the Van Alstyne fans. This trip would offer his only opportunity to swing the bat on the day. On the first pitch, Kelly drove a single to left center, scoring Mark Kackley and Armando Avina with the tying and winning runs respectively, causing Donnie to be mobbed by his teammates between first and second base. The 3A State Championship stage had been set.

"Congratulations, Donnie." Kelly turned to see Cassie standing a few feet away.

Beside her was Curt Burns. Don extended his hand, "I'm Don."

"Curt," replied Burns shaking Kelly's hand. Cassie reached for Donnie and hugged him tightly. *Oh, Cassie, this just isn't fair.*

Curt was as advertised. He was humble and personable. Donnie watched them together and could tell that Cassie was happy. If the truth be told, he would have to admit it hurt a little to see the two of them together in person. After a ten minute conversation, they

said their goodbyes and Donnie headed for the bus back to the hotel.
....

Don rode the elevator down to the lobby of the Holiday Inn Express. He had noticed a semi-secluded area when the team arrived after the game. He smiled when he saw a chair by the lamp, empty. Don took a bottle of water from the small refrigerator labeled *Complimentary for Our Guests.* He sat in the brown leather chair, set his half empty bottle on the table holding the lamp, and opened his Bible. After reading for several minutes, Donnie took another drink and noticed that he wasn't alone. There was an Air Force Officer seated across from him reading the newspaper. Donnie recognized the insignia indicating the man was a Colonel.

When the two made eye contact, the officer nodded and said, "Good evening, Mr. Kelly." Donnie looked at the Colonel in stunned silence. "My name is Matthew Townsend. I'm stationed at Lackland in San Antonio. I have followed your season and took this opportunity to meet James Kelly's boy.

"You knew my father, sir?" Townsend smiled and handed Donnie a manila envelope. He reached inside and pulled out a 5x7 picture of a much younger James and Matthew, in their flight suits, standing next to their F16s.

While he studied the picture, Colonel Townsend informed Donnie that the photograph was taken very early in their flying careers. "Your father was an excellent pilot, son. He was even a better leader; a real difference maker."

Kelly placed the photo back into the envelope and reached to hand it back to Colonel Townsend. "It's yours, son. I have another picture of your father on my wall back at the base." The Colonel read the look on Don's face, "Don, I have to be upfront with you. I have ulterior motives for being here. Do you have time for a short story?"

Don looked at the Grandfather Clock near the fireplace. "Yes sir, I don't have to be in my room for another hour."

165

Townsend sat back into his seat and placed his hands on his knees. "I ran into your father in October and he told me about seeing you play football. I actually watched you play your last two games and was truly impressed." Don smiled. "I played at the Academy with the recruiting coordinator, Jeremiah Johnson. After seeing you play, and my knowing the character of your father, I emphatically encouraged Jeremiah to go after you. Since that time, I have received two phone calls from him. The first was on the day you decided to be a Falcon. The second was the night you were drafted by the Colorado Rockies.

"Coach Johnson called me and left a message congratulating me on being selected." informed Don.

"He is happy for you, but is personally disappointed. Jeremiah spent some time checking on you. He talked to coaches, administrators, teachers and even your tutor, Mrs. Fleming. He told me that, without exception, each person he talked to said you were nothing like they had ever seen." Don lowered his eyes, embarrassed by the description attributed to him. "We love that you are a great athlete, Don, but we are truly more interested in what kind of person you are. You are a Kelly, son, and the Kelly's are natural born leaders." The Colonel stood, prompting Donnie to do the same. "Mr. Kelly, you have earned your place in this time in history. Your father would be proud."

Chapter 47

Don was the first player to make it downstairs for the continental breakfast provided by the hotel. The dining room area was empty except for an elderly couple sitting by the window drinking coffee. He noticed the two were holding hands on top of the table, which prompted a smile from Don. After choosing his breakfast, Donnie sat at a table for two near the fireplace.

"Good morning, Kelly." Don looked up to see Coach Haynes with a bagel and a cup coffee in his hands. He sat down in the empty chair across from his player. "How's the finger?"

Kelly looked at the injured fingertip, "I tried all my grips, and it was tender. If it wasn't my middle finger, I think I would be able to pitch. "

"I figured as much. I was just hoping you would have a miraculous recovery," joked Haynes.

"Nobriga will be fine, coach. He's a competitor."

"Oh, I agree, Don. I'm truly not concerned about Nick. It would just be nice to have your number one draft pick on the mound, that's all. Speaking of the draft, I asked Mr. Campbell to wait to contact you until we were finished. You should hear from him tonight or tomorrow."

"Coach, I've been thinking...." Don was distracted by a teammate heading toward them.

"Oh, I see how it is. Have breakfast with the coach and he might let you play."

"You are a funny guy, Randall." Donnie stood up and pointed to his chair. "Here Robert, you can sit in my place. Everyone knows you're the biggest sycophant on the team."

"I'm a what?" asked Randall.

"Look it up Rob," said Kelly as he tossed his trash in the can and headed for the elevator.

Don climbed the three steps on the charter bus for the short trip to the stadium. The Panthers were unaccustomed to traveling in style. Several local merchants chipped in to pay for the comfortable transportation. Donnie noticed Nick Nobriga sitting in the second seat, staring out the window, and sat down next to him. "What's on your mind, Nick?"

Nobriga turned toward Kelly revealing a concerned countenance. He looked around to see if anyone might be listening and quietly said, "I'm scared spitless, Donnie. The last thing I want to do is let this team down."

"How could you let us down?" asked Kelly.

"What if I pitch like crap?"

Don laughed and said, "Well, if you pitched like crap, then that would be the first time you did all year. I like the odds, Nick. Just throw strikes, and we will take care of the rest."

Kelly slapped Nobriga on the knee and headed toward his normal seat in the back of the bus. "Hey, Kelly." Don turned around and looked at his friend. "Thanks."

Don was prophetic with his promise to Nick. The Panthers turned four double plays in the 4-2 victory over the Glen Rose Tigers. Kelly was involved in nearly identical twin killings in the 1st and 4th innings. With the leadoff man on first, the number three hitter drove a ball into the right center gap for what appeared to be a sure double. Donnie overcame the distance between himself and the ball with an exceptional jump. He dove headlong into the gap, catching the ball and sliding several feet on the turf field. The surprised runner reversed course and sprinted back to first, only to be called out after Kelly's rocket-like throw beat him to the bag. Ironically, the same runner and hitter were involved in the 4th inning replay.

The Tiger's final out of the game was a routine fly ball to center. After catching the ball, Don started running to the forming

168

pile on the mound. When he reached the edge of the infield, his eye caught a glimpse of a man in Air Force dress blues, standing by himself at the top of the stadium. Donnie slowed to almost a walk, staring at the man who appeared to be staring back.

"Congratulations, son." Don turned toward the voice to find an umpire extending his hand to him. "Thank you, sir." After shaking the umpire's hand, Donnie directed his eyes back to the top of the stadium, only to find the airman gone.

. . . .

The charter rolled into Van Alstyne after the four hour trip from Round Rock. The noise level on the bus had coincided with the adrenaline drop in the players. Most ended up, either sleeping, or had headphones on, listening to music.

Coach Haynes was nodding off himself, when Donnie sat next to him. "Sorry to disturb you, Coach."

Jimmy yawned and stretched. "It's okay. It happens when you get my age."

Don smiled and continued. "I just wanted to thank you for everything coach. You and the other coaches have been there for me when I had no one. Coach Miller always says that you all loved us and would be there for us. Well, I can say that that wasn't just talk."

"You know, Don, I've been coaching a long time and can say that this group of coaches believes coaching is more of a calling than a profession."

Pressing on, Donnie said, "Coach, can I talk to you about something?....." They talked until the bus rolled into the Forrest Moore parking lot.

As he stepped off the bus, Coach Haynes ended the conversation. "Don, trust the way you were raised. You'll find your answer."

Chapter 48

Donnie sat in the Ole Miss rocking chair watching a male cardinal retrieve seeds from his Mimi's bird feeder and then feed them to his female mate. He had enjoyed watching these same two lovers over the past two years. His attention was diverted to the expected visitor coming up his drive.

Don stood and walked to the edge of the porch. Coach Jaycee Guerrero exited his vehicle and walked around to the other side to open the door for his beautiful new bride.

"Don, I would like to introduce you to my wife Ashley. Ashley, this is Don Kelly."

After exchanging pleasantries, Don took the newlyweds on a tour of the property. "I love your place Don," said the demure blonde. "It reminds me of my grandparent's house in East Texas."

"It sure beats our small apartment in town," added Jaycee.

Kelly reached into his pocket and pulled out three keys and handed them to Coach G. "These two are for the house, and this one is to the '69. Please drive her once in awhile."

"Are you kidding' me? I've been wanting to drive that bad boy since the first time I laid eyes on it!"

Don smiled, then continued with the final instructions. "All the fishing gear is in the back of the Gator."

"I love to fish," interjected Ashley.

"Well, that's something I didn't know about you, sweetheart," admitted Jaycee.

"Oh, and I told Coach Miller that the guys could work the course if he wanted."

"Oh trust me, they'll use it!" assured Guerrero. Changing the subject, he asked, "Don, are you sure you don't want more than $350 a month?"

"No sir. The house is paid for, and that money will take care of the taxes. Besides, you are doing me a favor watching over Mimi's house." They walked together, in silence, to Don's truck.

As Kelly stepped into the cab, Jaycee patted him on the back and said, "Knock 'em dead, Don Kelly."

Donnie waved to his new tenants as he left the property, headed for the Mile High City. On the way out of town, Don stopped at Diamonds to say goodbye to Caren. He grabbed a blue backpack with a white *VA* stenciled on the front and ***Kelly*** on the back. Inside was Donnie's outfielder glove, a Texas 3A Baseball Championship shirt, and a new pair of batting gloves.

Donnie found her in the back stocking breakfast cereals, singing softly. "Hello, Caren."

"You scared me, Don Kelly!" exclaimed Caren as she hit him on the shoulder. Don laughed and rubbed his arm faking excruciating pain. "What are you doing here, Mr. Kelly?"

"I came to say good-bye, Miss Caren." Caren's smile disappeared at the news. Handing the backpack to Caren, "Would you give this to Charlie for me, please?"

Trying not to cry, Caren said, "I'm sorry, Donnie. I have to get back to work."

Not wanting to embarrass her anymore, he walked toward the front of the store. When he reached the end of the aisle, Donnie turned back toward Caren. "Would it be okay if I call you once in awhile?"

She shook her head in the affirmative. When Don turned away, the smile returned to Caren Korabek's face.

Chapter 49

The thirteen hour trip to Denver was interrupted twice: once by Donnie stopping in Wichita Falls to eat at the Burrito Shop, and the second was dinner and an overnight stay with the Herrera's in Pueblo.

Donnie's meeting with Steve Campbell was scheduled for noon at Coors Field. He looked at his watch when he pulled onto Blake Street. It was 11:30 when he parked his truck in a spot near the front entrance. Don could feel the warmth leave his hands as he entered an open gate. He decided to take advantage of the time to check out the stadium. As the field came into view, Donnie couldn't help but recall all of the times he dreamed of playing in a stadium like this, in front of thousands of fans.

His day dream was broken by the Rockies GM, "Don Kelly?"

Don turned to see a middle aged man wearing a Polo shirt with *Colorado Rockies* embroidered on the left chest. "Hello, I'm Steve Campbell. Let's go to my office. We can have lunch while we talk."

. . . .

"Well, ladies and gentlemen, this is something you don't see every day." The ESPN anchor continued: *"The Colorado Rockies first round draft pick, Don Kelly, has decided to honor his commitment to play football, and now, baseball at the United States Air Force Academy. His decision to forego a multi-million dollar signing bonus placed him in rare company."*

Rockies General Manager, Steve Campbell explained, *"I talked with him for well over an hour, trying to convince him to sign. But after hearing his story, it's honestly difficult to find fault in his reasoning. The fact that he drove all the way from Texas to Denver, just to inform me of his decision face to face, indicates the character*

172

of this young man. This is truly a blow to the organization, but we hold no ill will toward young Mr. Kelly."

Coach Jimmy Haynes turned off his TV and said in a low voice: "Godspeed, Don Kelly."

Made in the USA
San Bernardino, CA
20 January 2017